Light & Hope !

Gcina Mhlophe

Gcina Mhlophe was born in Hammarsdale in KwaZulu-Natal, where she lived happily with her paternal grandmother until she was ten, then was relocated to her mother's family in Mount Frere in the Eastern Cape. After completing her Matric at Mfundisweni High School, she went on holiday to Johannesburg in 1979 … and stayed for the next 21 years. She now lives happily in Durban by the sea with her husband Karl and their beloved daughter Khwezi – the morning star!

Love Child

Gcina Mhlophe

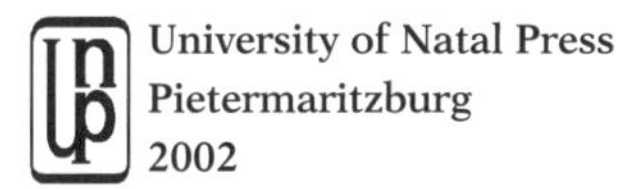
University of Natal Press
Pietermaritzburg
2002

Published by University of Natal Press
Private Bag X01, Scottsville 3209
South Africa
books@nu.ac.za

ISBN 1-86914-001-X

Edited by Elana Bregin

Cover photograph by Karl Becker

Cover design by Sumayya Essack, Dizzy Blue Dezign

Layout by Manoj Sookai

Printed and bound by Interpak Books, Pietermaritzburg

Contents

FOREWORD

This collection is very much a representative portrait of my work. Many of the poems and stories in it are known all over South Africa, and also in other countries where I have published and performed a lot. Some of these pieces have even been performed by others. And it's been great to have the chance to put together this journey of my life's experiences. To look back at these almost forgotten writings after so many years and wonder – did I say that?

The opening piece – 'Transforming Moments' – was inspired by a question that an editor once asked me: 'What helped to create the writer that you are?' At the time, I couldn't take time off from my performance schedule to answer it, so I didn't do anything about it for a year. But the question stayed in my mind. And late one night, I simply had to make the journey down memory lane, stopping often to ponder over the events of the formative years of my life. The curious thing for me, is that words have always been an important part of my life. Long before I set foot in school. Long before I ever imagined that I could even attempt to write. It was my grandmother who was the source of my love affair with words. She told me so many stories, sang me songs that taught my imagination to fly very early in my life. That was lucky for me!

The poem 'In the Company of Words' is really the story of who I am, told in the shortest possible way. When I perform it to a live audience, it feels like I am introducing myself as honestly as can be. Talking of performance poetry – I was introduced to the writing world by many great performers, storytellers, praise poets and preachers. So it was really just a matter of time before I too would find a live platform from which to present my work. My family and friends have always played a very central part in my writing, appearing in almost every story or poem. Even when the people that I write about are not directly family or friends, they are people with whom I feel a very strong connection – they either take me into their world, or I adopt them into mine. I don't have the correct term for this kind of writing, but I would call it intimate and personal. But hey – analysing things is one of my greatest difficulties, so let me stop right here!

Stories like 'The Toilet' and 'My Dear Madam' certainly take me back to a time that was difficult and frustrating beyond words. Then again, they not only remind me of where I come from, but also say to me that hope has always been my walking stick. The fact that I had no formal training in any of the jobs I ended up doing meant that I had to bear in mind an old Zulu saying that my father taught us as children – '*ayikho inkomo yobuthongo.*' It means, 'you can never earn a cow through sleeping.' That's why hard work became my middle name – and still is.

Through my writing, I have have also been able to work out many emotional wrangles and somehow find peace in my heart, even if the piece concerned was not publishable. A story like 'Crocodile Spirit', like so many others, was based on reality. It helped me to deal with the 1968 forced removals in my home town of Hammarsdale. The actual wooden crocodile that I refer to has been on the veranda of my father's home for as long as I can remember. Today, my father is too old to really take good care of it like he did before. But I can't imagine going home and not finding that crocodile there, with all the stories that it brings to mind ...

'Dumisani' was a young boy whom I knew nothing about,

until I met his mother and interviewed her; then, he went straight into my heart and stayed there. He was so gentle, harmless and instantly likeable, despite the horrors he had to go through so early on in his life. Today, I find myself wondering how he is; did he fully recover, is he a happy young man, with a family even? I wonder too about his mother, whose story I told so often in a theatre piece during the height of the 1986 State of Emergency. It was 'Born in the RSA', directed by Barney Simon of the Market Theatre. I think of the many times I stood back-stage before a performance, praying that I would have the ability to do justice to the story of a woman who did not have the privilege of standing in front of local and international audiences to tell it herself. When I received the OBBIE Award (an off-Broadway theatre award) for Best Actress, in New York, I felt strongly that it was also her award, together with many other women like her.

'Praise to Our Mothers', 'We Are at War', 'Say No' and 'Sitting Alone Thinking' all happened around that same time too, when the South African police ruled this country – or so it seemed to us, who were so heavily affected. We hardly slept at night. We kept our banned books under our mattresses and in other hidden places, for fear of those famous pre-dawn raids. But no matter how hot the political situation, or how daunting the other challenges of life, my childhood experiences managed to find their way into my writing somehow.

My mother's death was another very difficult time for me. I spent long periods in painful remembering, trying to bring back the times I had spent with her, the good as well as the bad. I sat alone in my hostel room for weeks and months on end, crying my eyes out, wishing that things could have been different between us, wishing we could talk now, wishing for so many things. 'Sweet Honey Nights' is my testimony to her and those painful, bitter-sweet years with her in the Eastern Cape. I'd been unwillingly relocated there at the age of ten, forced to leave behind my happy home with my beloved grandmother in KwaZulu-Natal. It was a time which for me was very unhappy –

eight long years spent in a constant state of longing for the home I had been torn from. It was only in retrospect that I realised how much of my creative voice was awakened during those difficult years, and how much of my writing self was set in motion then. At the time, my chronic homesickness was all I could see.

I wrote down many of my memories from that time, both good and bad. 'Nokulunga's Wedding' is one of these, based on the real experience of somebody close to me. The story terrified me when I heard it, and left me with a complete fear that the same fate would be mine. It says a lot about the poor state of male/female relations in the Mount Frere and other similar districts, which, in the year 2002, haven't improved much.

Also in my mother's village, lived a woman whom I remember very well. I was new in the village, I didn't speak Xhosa at that time, and the children there loved teasing me about the many things that they found funny about me. I observed a lot and learned fast. The woman I refer to is in this collection as 'Nongenile'. She was certainly very different! I don't know if she was 'not all there upstairs', but it seemed to me that she was like the village fool. Everyone treated her unfairly and no one took her seriously at all. She had two grown-up sons, but no husband or other known man in her life. She just did not fit in, and she was looked down upon as more inferior than the poorest person in the village. But she could thatch roofs very well and she had the energy of an ox. Whenever people needed somebody to carry a heavy load from town or wherever, she was the one they asked. It was quite a sight to see her running back to the village with the heavy load on her head, sweat pouring down her face and a big smile showing off those light brown teeth of hers. Her cracked feet made a pounding sound on the ground as she ran. This woman was one of the first people that I became interested in, since I too felt like an outsider there.

The Methodist Church in the village was one of the most popular churches in the area, and I loved going. The singing on its own always made me very happy. But there were also other unforgettable experiences in the church sometimes, and these would find their way into my writing too; like the old man who kept us enthralled with his praying. We children did not close our eyes, but watched the 'performance' with great excitement. Often, we went out and imitated him when no adults were about. His singing voice was unforgettable too, and so for us, his mere presence made our Sundays special. I 'fell in love with an old man's prayer' indeed!

In my nineteen years of international travelling, I've been to many exciting places and had some very memorable experiences; they'll be part of another book one day. But one of those times that stands out for me is the performance of 'Love Child'. I'd written it in reaction to the senseless 'Zulu–Xhosa War' (sparked off by conflict between Inkatha and ANC supporters) which I read about in the papers and heard or saw on the radio and TV news everyday. The violence of the early '90s was just horrendous – the darkest hour before dawn in our country's history. But it was not just a question of Zulu people killing Xhosa-speakers, end of story. A paid gunman walking into a packed train and shooting at random could never have known who among those passengers was Xhosa, who was Zulu, Sotho, or anything else. But the crazy simplification of the situation continued nonetheless.

I am a love child myself, having been born of a Xhosa mother and a Zulu father, and there are countless other such unions here and around the world. The magic drum in the story is, to me, a symbol representing the artistic community in South Africa. Through the arts, we were able to open doors, bring together people who would not even have thought of coming together under other circumstances. We represented our country overseas at a time when the media was banned and many of our leaders were in jail all over South Africa. It was a time when I lost several good friends in the space of two weeks, courtesy of the SAP (South African Police). A time when I was constantly chasing hatred out of my own heart, as I too had to face the bullets. The other stories that wrote themselves in accompaniment to 'Love Child' were about the everyday experiences of that time, and no matter how hard I tried to leave them out, they woke me up at night, shouting, 'What about me? I'm a story too, why not tell people about me!' So I had no choice but to include them.

Now you know why 'Love Child' had to be part of this collection. That drum in the story is more than just a drum; it's the first peace drum to be heard on this continent of ours. Its spirit is connected to all the other drums we hear around us today – the umbilical cord that binds us together in a circular dance under the moonlight. And as the women of this continent take their rightful place alongside their men, there is a new dawn slowly breaking.

I say all this while fully aware of the terrifying times we live in, in this year of 2002, with its HIV/AIDS, its thousands of child rape cases, both reported and unreported, its high incidence of woman abuse and old people debasement; all of this throwing a terrible blanket of shame over any achievements of victory we might wish to highlight. Is this the freedom we envisaged and fought for? So much poverty, corruption and crime. I'm afraid not! But this is the challenge of our present millennium. We are called to work, each one of us; like soldiers, we must serve our country, just as we did before. It's obvious that the struggle is far from over. Everyone remember that!

Gcina Mhlophe

Transforming Moments

I was seventeen years old and feeling very unsure of myself. With my school work, I was doing exceptionally well and most of the teachers at the high school loved me – or they seemed to. My essays were the epitome of good work and they would be read to the whole class. I was probably proud of myself, even though I didn't really give it any serious thought. Somehow, my academic success did not do much for my confidence or give me any self-love. I thought I was very ugly and the fact that my hair was so hard to manage did not make things easier. I used to describe it as dry grass in winter. After a while, I even stopped combing it. I'd wash it and dry it, get dressed in my black skirt and white shirt, which were not as nice as those of the other girls, and off I'd go to school. To top it all, I had knock-knees and big feet! I was just so ugly and awkward – I hated myself. And, my God – I sat in the front desk! Miss-ugly-top-of-the-class.

Our school was one of the biggest high schools in the Eastern Cape and we had a great school choir that simply collected trophies. I remember Bulelwa's voice every time I think of our choir. I used to close my eyes and enjoy listening to her sing. I don't know how many times I wished I had a tape recorder so that I could tape her voice and have the pleasure of listening to her for the rest of my life. I must say, I felt great on those rare afternoons when Bulelwa would come and study with me under the black wattle tree near the teachers' cottages. I loved that spot. And I also remember that Bulelwa would stand by me when some of the girls in our dormitory teased me about boys. They knew I was not very interested in boys and they would go on: 'But who would want to go out with her? She doesn't even try to look good!'

I remember this good-looking boy from Port Elizabeth who played rugby. It was half-way through the year and he still did not have a girlfriend. He was the star of our rugby team. I knew his name and I'd heard lots about how good he was, but I didn't really know him – I was not one to go to the sports field. I was forever buried in my books. I read all the prescribed books for my year and then I read any other book or newspaper or magazine that I could get my hands on. I read love stories by Barbara Cartland and Catherine Cookson; I read James Baldwin ... I read so much you'd think that was the only thing that kept me alive. Often, by the time the teacher came to do certain books in class, I had long since finished them and was wishing we'd move on to something I didn't know. Boys in my class did not like me very much – except when they needed help with school work. But with Maths we all relied on one particular boy who scared me a lot. Sometimes the Maths genius did help us when he felt like it.

In the girls' dormitory, my bed was at the far corner, away from the entrance and far enough from the Matron too. So, long after the lights were switched off, my deep voice could be heard droning away, doing what we had termed 'coughing'; I used to 'cough' out chapters and chapters of our set books and history syllabus to my classmates, who'd generally left it too late to do their school work and prepare for whatever big test was round the corner. While I helped them out, it was also useful to me to do the 'coughing'. It helped to jog my memory, as generally, some time would have elapsed since I had read the set book, subsequently becoming engrossed in others that had nothing to do with the syllabus. Because of the 'coughing', some of the girls were forced to be my part-time friends. Then came the day when we were rehearsing a new school play and the boy from Port Elizabeth walked up to me and told me that he loved me and wished that I would try to love him too.

Well, I thought he was crazy! What did a good-looking boy like that want with me – and besides, I went to that school to study, not to sleep with boys! I told him so. He tried to convince me that he did not mean to rush things; I did not have to sleep with him – he just liked me and he wanted to be my boyfriend. He said he really wanted to spend time with me and we could have good times together talking and reading, if that's what I wanted too. I asked him to please leave me alone.

Well, the Port Elizabeth boy didn't leave me alone, but many of the girls did. They thought he was too good for me. They claimed he was a city boy and should therefore go for a city girl. There were many remarks too, that I was ugly and did not have any fashionable clothes. Many girls now looked the other way when I walked towards them, and many unkind remarks were whispered behind my back. At first this annoyed me; I told whoever would listen that I didn't want anything to do with the handsome city boy – they could have him. But the hostility grew worse and the boy continued to follow me around. And then I began to find it funny. I looked at the girls who hated me and I wondered what would happen if I decided to accept the Rugby Star as my boyfriend. Sometimes, I laughed alone as I imagined what they could be whispering about me. Then I thought – well, he's not blind, he can see that I'm ugly, he can see I don't have any fashionable clothes, he can see that I read too much. I thought, fine – I'll go out with him. He had chosen an unsuitable girl and set the whole school on fire. My English teacher thought it was really funny. He congratulated me for causing such a stir! It turned out that Sizwe, the Rugby Star, was a lovely person, and we'd become good friends by the time he left the school at the end of that year.

I carried on with my school work and continued to please my sister in Johannesburg – she was the one paying for my education. I could imagine her face glowing when she received my good results and I wished that I could be there to see it. I was doing my Standard Nine then, and we'd just come back for the second semester after the winter holidays. Life was all right, everything was going the same as it always had. I'm not quite sure how it started, but as time went on, I had the feeling that my minister, Father Fikeni, had a soft spot for me. But then, maybe I don't have to explain too much. I think everyone has somebody in their lives who seems to like them for no particular reason – just like that. Sure, I was always well behaved in church and I was one of the three girls who cut and arranged flowers for the church vases every Sunday morning. I had been kicked out of the school choir because my voice was too deep and I was impatiently told to sing tenor with the boys or leave. Everybody had laughed and I got the general feeling that my voice was not too good. So I left. That also added to my Miss-ugly-top-of-the-class image. But the minister insisted that I be in the church choir, despite my protestations that my voice was ugly. He said my voice was strong and resonant – not ugly. That's the first time I heard the word resonant, and I liked it; so I joined the church choir.

Then, there was this particular Friday afternoon; a group of lazy girls was walking back from school. The winter sun seemed as lazy as we were. We had just walked past the minister's house when a young boy ran up to tell me that Father Fikeni wanted to see me. I went with him and was about to walk into the kitchen, when the minister himself came out and gave me swift instructions to go and pack my weekend bag, because he and his wife were going to visit family in Tsolo and I was invited to come with them. I stood there at the top of the stairs open-mouthed, unable to move or speak. The minister looked at me and laughed out loud. He told me that we had less than an hour to go, so I should run. Without a word I turned and took all five steps in one big jump. Running at top speed, clutching my books tightly to my chest, I suddenly realised that I was not alone in the world – everyone was staring at me. I tried to pull myself together and put a hand across my lips to hide my enormous grin.

Once in my dormitory, I did not know what to take or leave; I was not exactly used to going away on weekends. I quickly changed out of my school uniform and into my best dress. I ran to the bathroom to wet my hair a little so I could try to comb it. It was too painful to do a proper job, but I sort of tugged and patted it down with my hand. When I thought it felt a bit better, I went and got my plastic bag with the few necessities for the weekend. I realised I had forgotten my nighty and hurried to get it from under my pillow. People were following me around, curious, but too proud to ask what was going on. I was not going to say a word till they asked!

Finally, Nosisa grabbed me by the arm just as I was walking out the door. 'Aren't you going to tell us where you're going?'

That opened the way for everyone to ask me questions, all at the same time.

'I'm going with Father Fikeni to visit his family for the weekend; he said I must run,' was all I told them.

With that, I pulled my arm free and walked quickly out of the gate.

The drive to Tsolo was relaxing, with the sun setting ahead of us and me dreaming away in the back seat. The minister and his wife sat in front and they seemed to be at peace with themselves. Mrs Fikeni was a beautiful lady who did not talk too much. Many times in church, I would look at her and wish that some angel would come into the church and ask me what I wanted. I knew exactly what I would ask for – I wanted to be as beautiful as the minister's wife.

That night, we went to bed at about ten, after the evening prayer. I fell asleep very quickly; maybe I was tired out from all my excitement. I was still excited when I woke up the next morning, to realise that no bells rang here to command me to wake up or go to the dining hall or school. I had a shower and went to help out in the kitchen. I liked the fact that I was not treated like some special guest who couldn't even do the dishes. I felt very much at home.

A short while after breakfast, we were all sitting on the veranda drinking some tea, with me seated next to the minister's wife. She was knitting a huge jersey with red and blue stripes. It looked so big that I doubted it was hers, but she assured me it was – she said she liked it that way, long and big like a coat. I sat there, content, staring at her fast moving hands and glancing every now and then into her face. It was as relaxed and beautiful as ever. She hardly even looked at her knitting, except when she ran out of wool or when she had to change colour. We were still sitting like that when Father Fikeni stood up, stretched his arms and said that it was time to go. Time to go where? I wondered, but only half-heartedly, still absorbed by his wife's busy hands. Presently, feeling his eyes on me, I looked up. Smiling, the minister suggested that I might like to go with him. He said he had a surprise for me. I searched his face hopefully for a clue. But it gave nothing away. All he said, as I followed him into the house, was that he was going to a meeting and he thought I might be interested in seeing what goes on at such occasions. There was nothing for me to do but swallow my curiosity and get ready to go.

The meeting was held at a nearby village, at the chief's place. It was very well attended. Looking at all the people sitting on the grass, on rocks or wooden stools near the cattle kraal, I decided that the whole village must have turned out for the occasion. We were late arrivals, but no one seemed to be too concerned. They made space for us to sit, while the speaker carried on and the people listened. I remember he was saying something about allowing cattle into the mealie fields, but only by agreement of all the people, and only once everyone had finished reaping their crops. His suggestion was something along those lines. More people participated in the discussion that followed, which didn't seem to have much to do with me at all. I sat there quietly, trying to be interested, but not succeeding too well. And then, all of a sudden, this man – tall, with big shoulders and a very dark face – leaped up from the crowd, his eyes flashing this way and that way, as if he was on the alert for something. He wore a beautifully made dark red hat with beads and a long black feather on it. He had more beads around his neck and waist. And a leather skirt, with the front part reaching just above the knees and the back much longer and flowing behind. He carried a strong-looking short stick, with the tip made longer by a white oxtail attached to it. He held it in one hand and in the other, he had a big, red, almost blanket-like cloth, thrown casually over his arm. Everyone sat up expectantly. Father Fikeni looked at me with a big smile. The look in his eyes told me: 'This is your surprise now – enjoy!'

The brightly dressed man started off by singing the praises of the chief's family, and then he sang about the chief's achievements, about the village people and about the great heroes of the past and present. His use of language was pure and flowing – and so were his movements. He leapt forward and hit the ground with his oxtail stick, hardly making a sound; I saw some people unconsciously imitating him. One minute, he would be praising, the next, he was reflective and critical. I had heard of *imbongi* – a praise poet – but I'd never dreamt that I'd see one in action. I was staring open-mouthed; even today, looking back, I still don't know exactly how to describe the feeling I had then. I only remember that when the man had finished and people moved forward to congratulate him, I was too tired to even clap my hands or join in the ululation and whistles ... I simply sat there, and in my dreamy mind, saw myself in similar attire, doing what I had just seen the man do. I made my decision there and then that I was also a praise poet. That was a beautiful moment for me, to think of myself in that way. I shook a few people's hands and the minister introduced me to the chief, who thanked him for coming and laughingly asked what I was doing at such a meeting. And then the *imbongi* came to greet Father Fikeni. After their longish chat, I was introduced to him as a very good student – during which time I was frozen and dumb from disbelief and God knows what else. As I felt the poet's hot, sweaty hand holding mine, I felt baptised as a poet too. I think I wanted to say something clever, but all I could do at that moment was smile and fidget with my button-holes. The poet went on to talk with other people, who called him Cira.

It was a Monday afternoon and I was lying on my stomach in my favourite spot under the black wattle trees when I wrote my first poem. I'd never had a child, but the great feeling that swept over me then was too overwhelming for words; I wondered whether that's how people feel when they have their first baby. I sat up and read it out loud. I liked the sound of my own voice, and I liked hearing the poem. I put the paper down and ran my fingers over my face to feel my features – the smile that wouldn't leave my face, my nose, my cheekbones, my eyes, my ears – including the pointy parts at the top that made my ears look like cups; I even felt my hair and I liked that too. For the first time, I liked the texture of my hard curly hair and my face didn't feel so ugly – everything just felt fine. My voice sounded like it was a special voice, made specially to recite poems with dignity. Resonant – was that it? That's the day I fell in love with myself; everything about me was just perfect.

I collected my books and the towel I was lying on, stood up and stretched my limbs. I felt tall and fit. I felt like jumping and laughing until I could not laugh anymore. I wanted tomorrow to come so that I could go and buy myself a new notebook to write my poems in. A woman praise poet – I'd never heard of one, but what did it matter? I could be the first one! I knew Father Fikeni would agree with me. I couldn't wait to see his face when I read him my poem. Across the fence, a big red cock flapped its wings and crowed loudly at me, as if in agreement.

In the Company of Words

It is truly marvellous, wonderful and comforting
To know that I have eyes to read
Hands that can write
And an enormous love for words
I am lucky to be speaking a few extremely beautiful languages
For I love words – language's ancestor
When I'm happy, words define my happiness
When I'm sad and confused
Words turn into clay and allow me
To mould and remould my muddled-up thoughts
Till I find inner peace in my soul

Had I to choose between weeping and reading
I'd most definitely choose reading
A good book
For I have proof, for aches and tensions
It works!
Countless times I've turned my back on pain
And found friends in characters from far-off lands
Countless times I've defied anger
And caressed my nerves with an old comic book
Countless nights I've triumphed over insomnia
And had a heart to heart talk with my pen and paper

I come to my desk in the dead of the night
I sit, without a clue as to how I wish to start
But then, before I know it, words of all types and sizes
Come rushing into my fingertips
As I feel my whole body smile
I welcome them, every single one of them
Like the good old friends that they are
When they start dancing in large circles around me
Throwing teasing wordy circles on my walls
I am convinced that I was not born to be bored
For how indeed can boredom even begin to penetrate
My timeless word circle
Now you see why I'm so content
In the company of words

The Toilet

Sometimes I wanted to give up and be a good girl who listened to her elders. Maybe I should have done something like teaching or nursing as my mother wished. People thought these professions were respectable, but I knew I wanted something different, though I was not sure what. I thought a lot about acting ... My mother said that it had been a waste of good money educating me, because I did not know what to do with the knowledge I had acquired. I'd come to Johannesburg for the December holidays after writing my Matric exams, and then stayed on, hoping to find something to do. My elder sister worked in Orange Grove as a domestic worker, and I stayed with her in her back room. I didn't know anybody in Jo'burg except my sister's friends, with whom we went to church. The Methodist Church up Fourteenth Avenue was about the only outing we had together. I was very bored and lonely.

On weekdays, I was locked in my sister's room so that the Madam wouldn't see me. She was at home most of the time: painting her nails, having tea with friends, or lying in the sun by the swimming pool. The swimming pool was very nearby the room, which is why I had to keep very quiet. My sister felt bad about locking me in there, but she had no alternative. I couldn't even play the radio, so she brought me books, old magazines and newspapers from the white people. I just read every single thing I came across: *Fair Lady*, *Woman's Weekly*, anything. But then my sister thought I was reading too much.

'What kind of wife will you make if you can't even make baby clothes, or knit yourself a jersey? I suppose you will marry an educated man like yourself, who won't mind going to bed with a book and an empty stomach.'

We would play cards at night when she knocked off, and listen to the radio, singing along softly with the songs we liked.

Then I got this temporary job in a clothing factory in town. I looked forward to meeting new people and liked the idea of being out of that room for a change. The factories made clothes for ladies' boutiques.

The whole place was full of machines of all kinds. Some people were sewing, others were ironing with big heavy irons that pressed with a lot of steam. I had to cut all the loose threads that hang after a dress or a jacket is finished. As soon as a number of dresses in a certain style was finished, they would be sent to me and I had to count them, write the number down, and then start with the cutting of the threads. I was fascinated to discover that one person made only sleeves, another the collars and so on, until the last lady put all the pieces together, sewed on buttons or whatever was necessary to finish.

Most people at the factory spoke Sotho, but they were nice to me – they tried to speak to me in Zulu or Xhosa, and they gave me all kinds of advice on things I didn't know. There was this girl, Gwendolene – she thought I was very stupid. She called me a 'bari' because I always sat inside the changing room with something to read when it was time to eat my lunch, instead of going outside to meet guys. She told me it was cheaper to get myself a 'lunch boy' – somebody to buy me lunch. She told me it was wise not to sleep with him, because then I could dump him anytime I wanted to. I was very nervous about such things. I thought it was better to be a 'bari' than to be stabbed by a city boy for his money.

The factory knocked off at four-thirty, and then I went to a park near where my sister worked. I waited there till half past six, when I could sneak into the house again without the white people seeing me. I had to leave the house before half past five in the mornings as well. That meant I had to find something to do with the time I had before I could catch the seven-thirty bus to work – about two hours. I would go to a public toilet in the park. For some reason it was never locked, so I would go in and sit on the toilet seat and read some magazine or other until the right time to catch the bus.

The first time I went into this toilet, I was on my way to the bus stop. Usually, I went straight to the bus stop outside the OK Bazaars, where it was well lit and I could see. I would wait there, reading or just looking at the growing number of cars and buses on their way to town. On this day, it was raining quite hard, so I thought I would shelter in the toilet until the rain passed. I knocked first to see if there was anybody inside. As there was no reply, I pushed the door open and went in. It smelled a little – a dryish kind of smell, as if the toilet was not used all that often. But it was quite clean compared to many 'Non-European' toilets I knew. The floor was painted red and the walls were cream-white. It did not look like it had been painted for a few years. I stood looking around, with the rain coming down very hard on the zinc roof. The noise was comforting – to know I had escaped the wet, only a few heavy drops had got me. The plastic bag in which I carried my book, purse and neatly folded pink handkerchief was a little damp, but that was because I had used it to cover my head when I ran to the toilet. I pulled my dress down a little so that it would not get creased when I sat down. The closed lid of that toilet was going to be my seat for many mornings after that.

I was really lucky to have found that toilet, because the winter was very cold. Not that it was any warmer in there, but once I'd closed the door it was at least a little less windy. Also, the toilet was very small – the walls were wonderfully close to me – it felt like it was made to fit me alone. I enjoyed that kind of privacy. I did a lot of thinking while I sat on that toilet seat. I did a lot of daydreaming too – many times imagining myself in some big hall doing a really popular play with other young actors. At school, we took set books like *Buzani kuBawo* or *A Man for All Seasons* and made school plays which we toured to the other schools on weekends. I loved it very much. When I was even younger, I had done little sketches taken from the Bible and on big days like Good Friday, we acted and sang happily.

I would sit there dreaming …

I was getting bored with the books I was reading – the love stories all sounded the same, and besides that I just lost interest. I started asking myself why I had not written anything since I left school. At least at school, I had written a few poems or stories for the school magazine, school competitions or other magazines like *Bona* and *Inkqubela*. Our English teacher was always so encouraging; I remembered the day I showed him my first poem – I was so excited I couldn't concentrate in class for the whole day. I didn't know anything about publishing then, and I didn't ask myself if my stories were good enough. I just enjoyed writing things down when I had the time. So one Friday, after I'd started being that toilet's best customer, I bought myself a notebook in which I was hoping to write something. I didn't use it for quite a while; until one evening …

My sister had taken her usual Thursday afternoon off, and she had been delayed somewhere. I came back from work, then waited in the park for the right time to go back into the yard. The white people always had their supper at six-thirty and that was the time I used to steal my way in without disturbing them or being seen. My comings and goings had to be secret, because they still didn't know I stayed there.

Then I realised that my sister hadn't come back. I was scared to go out again, in case something went wrong this time, so I decided to sit down in front of my sister's room, where I thought I wouldn't be noticed. I was reading a copy of *Drum Magazine* and hoping that she would come back soon – before the dogs sniffed me out. For the first time, I realised how stupid it was of me not to have cut myself a spare key long ago. I kept on hearing noises that sounded like the gate opening. A few times, I was sure I had heard her footsteps on the concrete steps leading to the servants' quarters, but each time it turned out to be something or someone else.

I was trying hard to concentrate on my reading again, when I heard the two dogs playing, chasing each other nearer and nearer to where I was sitting. And then they were in front of me, looking as surprised as I was. For a brief moment we stared at each other, then they started to bark at me. I was sure they would tear me to pieces if I moved just one finger, so I sat very still, trying not to look at them, while my heart pounded and my mouth went dry as paper.

They barked even louder when the dogs from next door joined in, glaring at me through the openings in the hedge. Then the Madam's high-pitched voice rang out above the dogs' barking.

'Ireeeeeeeene!' That's my sister's English name, which we never use. I couldn't move or answer the call – the dogs were standing right in front of me, their teeth so threateningly long. When there was no reply, she came to see what was going on.

'Oh, it's you? Hello.' She was smiling at me, chewing that gum which never left her mouth, instead of calling the dogs away from me. They had stopped barking, but they hadn't moved – they were still growling at me, waiting for her to tell them what to do.

'Please Madam, the dogs will bite me,' I pleaded, not moving my eyes from them.

'No, they won't bite you.' Then she spoke to them nicely, 'Get away now – go on,' and they went off.

She was like a doll, her hair almost orange in colour, all curls round her made-up face. Her eyelashes fluttered like a doll's. Her thin lips were bright red, like her long nails, and she wore very high-heeled shoes. She was still smiling; I wondered if it didn't hurt after a while. When her friends came for a swim, I could always hear her forever laughing at something or other.

She scared me – I couldn't understand how she could smile like that but not want me to stay in her house.

'When did you come in? We didn't see you.'

'I've been here for some time now – my sister isn't here. I'm waiting to talk to her.'

'Oh – she's not here?' She was laughing, for no reason that I could see. 'I can give her a message – you go on home – I'll tell her that you want to see her.'

Once I was outside the gate, I didn't know what to do or where to go. I walked slowly, kicking my heels. The street lights were so very bright! Like big eyes staring at me. I wondered what the people who saw me thought I was doing, walking around at that time of the night. But then I didn't really care, because there wasn't much I could do about the situation right then. I was just thinking how things had to go wrong on that day particularly, because my sister and I were not on such good terms. Early that morning, when the alarm had gone for me to wake up, I did not jump to turn it off, so my sister got really angry with me. She had gone on about me always leaving it to ring for too long, as if it was set for her, not for me. And when I went out to wash, I had left the door open a second too long and that was enough to earn me another scolding.

Every morning I had to wake up straight away, roll my bedding and put it under the bed where my sister was sleeping. I was not supposed to put on the light, although it was still dark. I'd light up a candle and tiptoe my way out with a soap dish and a toothbrush. My clothes were on a hanger on a nail at the back of the door. I'd take the hanger and close the door as quietly as I could. Everything had to be set ready the night before. A basin full of cold water was also ready outside the door, put there because the sound of running water and the loud screech the taps made in the morning could wake up the white people, and they would wonder what my sister was doing up so early. I'd do everything and be off the premises by five-thirty with my shoes in my bag – I only put them on once I was safely out of the gate. And that gate made such a noise too.

Many times I wished I could jump over it and save myself all that sickening careful-careful business!

Thinking about all these things took my mind away from the biting cold of the night and my wet nose, until I saw my sister walking towards me.

'Mholo, what are you doing outside in the street?' she greeted me. I quickly briefed her on what had happened.

'Oh Yehovah! You can be so dumb sometimes! What were you doing inside in the first place? You know you should have waited for me so we could walk in together. Then I could say you were visiting or something. Now, you tell me, what am I supposed to say to them if they see you come in again? Hayi!'

She walked angrily towards the gate, with me hesitantly following her. When she opened the gate, she turned to me with an impatient whisper.

'And now? Why don't you come in, stupid?'

I mumbled my apologies, and followed her in. By some miracle, no one seemed to have noticed us. We quickly munched a snack of cold chicken and boiled potatoes and drank our tea, hardly on speaking terms. I wanted to just howl like a dog. I wished somebody would come and be my friend, and tell me that I was not useless, and that my sister did not hate me, and that one day I would have a nice place to live ... anything. It would have been really great to have someone my own age to talk to. But I also knew that my sister was worried for me and she was scared of her employers. If they were to find out that I lived with her, they would fire her, and then we would both be walking up and down the streets. My R11.00 wages weren't going to help us at all. I don't know how long I lay like that, unable to fall asleep, just wishing and wishing as the tears ran into my ears.

The next morning, I woke up long before the alarm went off, but I just lay there, feeling tired and depressed. If there had been a way out, I wouldn't have gone to work. But there was also this other strong feeling or longing inside me. It was some kind of pain, that pushed me to do everything at double speed and run off to my toilet. I call it 'my toilet' because that is exactly how I felt about it. It was very rarely that I ever saw anybody else go in there in the mornings. It was as if they all knew I was using it, and they had to lay off or something. When I went there, I didn't really expect to find it occupied.

I felt my spirits lifting as I put on my shoes outside the gate. I made sure that my notebook was in my bag. In my haste, I even forgot my lunch-box, but it didn't matter. I was walking faster and my feet were feeling lighter all the time. Then I noticed that the door had been painted and that a new window pane had replaced the old broken one. I smiled to myself as I reached the door. Before long, I was sitting on that toilet seat, writing a poem.

Many more mornings saw me sitting there, writing. Sometimes it did not need to be a poem; I wrote anything that came into my head – in the same way I would have done if I'd had a friend to talk to. I remember some days when I felt like I was hiding something from my sister. She didn't know about my toilet in the park and she was not in the least interested in my notebook.

Then, one morning, I wanted to write a story about what had happened at work the day before; the supervisor screaming at me for not calling her when I'd seen people stealing two dresses at lunch-time. I had found it really funny. I had to write about it and I just hoped there were enough pages left in my notebook. It all came back to me and I was smiling when I reached for the door; but it wouldn't open – it was locked! I think for the first time, I accepted that the toilet was not mine after all ...

Slowly I walked over to a bench nearby, watched the early spring sun come up, and wrote my story anyway.

Nongenile

My body was young
But I also remember
Now that I think about it
My mind was even younger
I smiled at everyone
I was the new girl from the East Coast
Learning a new language
And I did not know everyone's names

The first name to really stick in my mind
Was that of Mama Nongenile
Who lived alone five houses away
She talked to herself all day long
And she laughed out loud
And slapped the side of her thigh
Whenever anyone stopped and stared at her

People had a song about Nongenile
Which they sang as they chopped
Firewood in the forests of Ndlovini
Their bush knives coming down
Almost at the same time

Mama Nongenile knew of the song
It made her feel good
To hear the same people who looked down upon her
The same people who did not want their children
To go anywhere near her
As if she had a disease they could catch –
Just by sitting next to her
People who seemed to wish her dead
It made her feel good
To hear the same people sing about her

But to hear Mama Nongenile sing and dance
To her song at the harvest celebrations
Was, to me, the highlight of the season
I loved to watch her cracked feet
Come down to hit the ground – hard!
Then I waited for her to stop
Everything and everyone, and take control
She would walk up and down, back and forth
Staring daringly into people's eyes
Everyone had to listen
Listen to Mama Nongenile sing her praises
The only time anyone heard anything good
Said about her:
Ndangena mna Nongenile kwathul' umoya
Yangen' intombi ka Mahlathi Bhembe, kwakrakra mathe
emlonyeni
Intombi eyazalelwa esihlabathini solwandle eSajonisi
Kub' umama wayeyo qoqa onokrwece

'Here enters the daughter of Mhlathibhembe
Who was born at the beach in Port St. Johns
My mother went to collect seashells at the beach in Port St. Johns
And did not see that the weather was changing

Kanti akalibonanga ukuba izulu liyezisa
Ndahlanzwa ngamanzi olwandle
Ndaphuma ndimhle okwekhwezi lomso!

This is the time for Nongenile to speak
Speak to the people who avoid me
Unless they need me to carry heavy parcels
From their husbands in the big cities
People who need me to thatch their roofs
But never invite me back for a drink
Once the job is done

I do not eat children
You have no reason to worry
Please do not try to forget me while I still live
I'm not easy to forget
Long after I have died
You will hear my laugh echoing
Up in the hills across the big river
Long after I have died
I know the children of your children
Will hear my song and wonder
What I looked like
Maybe they will go high up in the hills
Calling my name
Their little hearts hoping
That I will come out
And teach them a happy new game

And the storm was gathering
She was thrown into the Ocean
And I was birthed by the Ocean
That's why I'm so beautiful, like the daybreak!'

Sweet Honey Nights

I spent many years trying
Trying to understand my mother
And I am sure she tried even harder
To understand me – her youngest daughter
We were so alike, and yet so different
A powerful river of determination
Ran in our blood
When she wanted something
Mama sure went for it
I do the same!
And I remember it was great
When both of us wanted the same thing
But when our wishes differed
The storm, the heavy rain of tears, and the pain
To this day I remember that well

After she died I realised that
My mind did not recall
Any of the good times
The pain and the tears filled my thoughts
Soon I knew I had to go back
Shake up the bones
And try to find the other stories
From the bones of memory

The grass from her grave was swaying
In the wind, whispering a quiet rhythm
For a long time I stood and listened
Lost to my immediate surroundings
Caught up in a time when I was very young
More playful and excitable than I am today

And then I think I heard a jawbone move
I felt my ear starting to itch
And I think I heard these words:
'Sweet honey nights, sweet honey nights
Winter times in the Eastern Cape
Close your eyes, remember the smell
And the taste of honey
Sweet honey nights, sweet honey nights
Smile a little, swallow once and the story is yours'

* * *

I have loved stories for as long as I can remember, told to me by my beloved grandmother. With her stories, she taught me to let my imagination fly, to imagine worlds under the sea, above the clouds, and to see trees, plants and living creatures that deserved respect, just like me. When I learned to read, I had access to even more stories. Books became my companions and I was forever hungry to learn new things. My love for books and words in whatever shape or size is well known to all who meet me. But something I have not given much thought to, is my love for honey. As a public performer, my voice often gets tired and I need to eat honey to soothe it. Recently, I dreamed about visiting my mother's grave and the whole story of my love for honey came back to me. I suddenly remembered it as if it had happened just the other day …

It was a cold winter's day and Mama had given each of us children chores to do, to keep us busy while she was away. She took a metal bucket, a towel and matches to light a fire. Then she set off on her own, not telling us where she was going. She was gone for hours. But we were so busy with our chores that we did not bother ourselves with trying to think where she might have gone. It was late afternoon when she returned, a satisfied smile playing about her lips. She put the bucket in the kitchen and kept it covered. We children were curious, but did not dare to ask what was in the bucket. Mama then told us to grab one of the many fat chickens running about outside and prepare it for supper.

We fetched some spring onions and herbs from the garden and added them into the pot. Quickly, we finished whatever we had to do outside, then hurried into the kitchen and closed the door. The fire was burning in the centre of the hut, the pots were cooking and it was warm and cosy. We listened to the cold wind howling outside and felt very good. The thatch grass on the roof always seems to keep the heat in very well when you need it to. I still love thatched roofs to this day. The smell of cooking meat, the quiet chatter amongst us children, and the promise of a particularly good supper was just wonderful. Mama was lost in her own world and hardly said a word. When the food was ready, my elder sister dished up and we all got down to the business of eating. We were sitting on the floor on grass mats and sheep skins, very comfortable. The food was delicious and our mouths were too busy to bother with conversation. It was quiet for some time until, one by one, we put away our plates, had a drink, and relaxed with a happy stomach and a satisfied look on our faces. We were all certain that we could not possibly take in any more food for the night. There simply was no space in our stomachs for anything else.

Mama slowly wiped her hands, looked at us mischievously and asked me to pick up the bucket and bring it to her. It was still covered with the towel, just as she had left it. I brought it to her. Dramatically, she removed the towel and a wonderful smell filled the room. Honey, that's what it was! She was simply unbelievable, my Mama! Her method of gathering honey always worked. She would go into the forest, all on her own, never taking anyone with her, returning without fail with a bucketful of delicious honey. The bees never seemed to give her any trouble. How did she do it?

Wide-eyed and full of anticipation, we suddenly felt our stomachs making space for what was to come. Each of us brought our plates to Mama so she could put a big, juicy honey-comb on it. We thanked her and sat down to enjoy the honey and chew the waxy bits. It was just wonderful; I remember vividly how I could simply not stop smiling. I was in Heaven, and nothing could make me happier.

I looked at my mother and felt a huge wave of love for her. I couldn't speak, even when she returned my gaze and asked if I wanted to say something. I just licked my lips and looked at my sweet, shiny hands and did not answer. Outside, the wind continued to howl, while we sat inside, savouring our sweet honey night.

You know something; in the mad times that I live in, surrounded by so much violent crime in the city of Johannesburg and other parts of South Africa, one really needs to have sweet memories like these. I certainly need my dreams of better times in the future. I have hope in my heart, because I know many people in this country who are working hard to make a difference one way or another. Working so much with young people as I do, I keep trying to add my own share of sweetness; little mouthfuls of honey, one spoon at a time …

Praise to Our Mothers

If the moon were to shine tonight
To light up my face and show off my proud form
With beads around my neck and shells in my hair
And a soft easy flowing dress with the colours of Africa

If I were to stand on top of a hill
And raise my voice in praise
Of the women of my country
Who have worked throughout their lives
Not for themselves but for the very life of all Africans
Who would I sing my praises to?
I could quote all the names, yes,
But where do I begin?!

Do I begin with the ones who gave their lives
So we others may live a better life
The Lilian Ngoyis, the Victoria Mxenges
The Ruth Firsts
Or the ones who lost their men to Robben Island
And their children to exile, but carried on fighting
The MaMotsoaledis, the MaSisulus
The Winnie Mandelas

Maybe I would sing my praises to the ones
Who had the resilience and cunning of a desert cobra
Priscila Jana, Fatima Meer, Beauty Mkhize
And those who turned deserts into green vegetable gardens
From which our people could eat
Mamphela Ramphele, Ellen Khuzwayo

Or would it be the names of the women who marched
Suffered solitary confinement and house arrests
Helen Joseph, Amina Cachalia, Sonya Bunting
Thoko Mngoma, Florence Matomela ...
How many more names come to mind
As I remember the defiance campaign
The fights against Beer Halls that suck the strength
Of our men
Building of alternative schools away from Bantu Education
And the fights against pass laws

Maybe I would choose a name
Just one special name that spells out light
That of Mama Nokukhanya Luthuli
Maybe if I were to call out her name
From the top of the hill
While the moon is shining bright:
NO-KU-KHA-NYA !
NO-KU-KHA–NYA !!!
Maybe my voice would be carried by the wind
To reach all the other women
Whose names are not often mentioned
The ones who sell oranges and potatoes
So their children can eat and learn
The ones who scrub floors and polish executive desktops
In towering office blocks
While the city sleeps
The ones who work in overcrowded hospitals
Saving lives, cleaning bullet wounds
and delivering new babies

And what about those who are stranded in 'Homelands'
With a baby in the belly and a baby on the back
While their men are sweating in the bowels of the earth
May the lives of all these women
Be celebrated and made to shine
When I call out Mama Nokukhanya's name
Because we who are young, salute our mothers
Who have given us the heritage
Of their Queendom!

My Dear Madam

On 24th February 1980, I was employed as a domestic servant. My madam was an English woman who lived in a small house by herself. Her children were in England and she was divorced from her husband. She was constantly on the phone, telling her friends about her 'new girl'.

She owned an antique shop just next door to her house, which was why she never bothered to stay in the shop. All the customers would come to the house and have a cup of tea or coffee and, of course, a friendly chat.

My madam was a very talkative somebody. It did not make a difference whether she knew a person or not, she would start telling him or her about this and that in her life. When she finally decided to take the customer to the shop, she would call me to follow her no matter what I was doing.

This was the case because all the girls she had employed before were bread snatchers. I was, according to her, a very good girl, but it seemed I was not exceptional or different where thieving was concerned. This made things difficult for me, because I could not rush through my work the way I wanted to.

To be honest, the house was quite small and because she was alone, there was not much ironing or washing. It was for this reason that she would sometimes take out a bundle of her clothes from the wardrobe so I could iron them. I think she carelessly bundled them up on purpose. I did not mind anyway. One problem I did mind, was that there was no Hoover for the floors, so I had to go down on my knees in every room every day. Anything like this that was missing, anything my dear madam did not have, she blamed on somebody, telling me that one girl or the other had either stolen or broken it. There was no lunch time at all. I had to quickly munch whatever she gave me and go on with my work. Because she was quite a fat lady, she was always sort of on diet, but she could not stick to it for more than two days before going back to her fattening foods again.

I felt sorry for her, but I could not help laughing when she said that one of her boyfriends wanted her to lose some weight.

'How are you going to do that?' I asked, laughing.

'I really don't know, but I must do it somehow. I love him,' she said, making faces at me, and it ended up being a joke. I knew as well as she did that she could not make it. Trying to lose weight was just a punishment for my dear madam.

The first two weeks with my madam were very happy ones. We were always talking about this and that in the world, about our likes and dislikes. Sometimes, she would tell me about her previous girls, who could not behave themselves.

'What did they do?' I asked.

'They would steal my clothes, my money and even pinch my powdered soap.'

'Mmm, that was bad of them.'

'Yes, yes, it was. I remember one girl even stole my bra, a momento from a friend of mine.'

I said, 'She must have been a fat girl, that one.'

She replied, 'Yes, she was, and very cheeky too.'

'Shame, they gave you a hard time, madam.'

So we would go on like that, and I felt sorry for my poor madam, especially when she appealed to me one day: 'Please do not steal my things. Honestly, I am saving to go to England as soon as possible and if you are still a good girl we can both fly to England and leave this mad country. How's that?'

She would say that jokingly, patting me on the shoulder like a little girl. I would just laugh at the idea. One time, she said I could even marry a Negro out there. My madam could really talk!

I could not make it to work at 7.30a.m. as she wished, so we changed things to eight o'clock. This, she understood, because I stayed far away and the buses were giving a lot of trouble. From the bus stop to her house was another ten minutes walk. The bus fare was a pain in the neck: R1.00 daily! Sometimes, I would be short of bus fare and then I had to rely on my sister, friends or anybody who did not mind giving me a few cents. My madam made it clear that she could not afford to help me, because she was saving money to take her back to her country, where her mother was very sick and unhappy.

She soon suggested that I should stay in the girl's room in the backyard. I was sort of interested in seeing this room. When I opened the door, a well-made desk which looked in good condition invited me in. The room itself was very small in the true sense of the word. I also saw a single bed with a very old three-quarter mattress on it. And a two-plate electric stove which, due to its old age, served as a bedside table. There was nothing else in the room. I looked up at the roof and it was black with soot. I could not help imagining how terrible it would be when it started to sweat (if that is the right word to use). All I know is that you would have to forget about your clothing once it got caught by those heavy black drops from the roof.

The wall was newly painted in a pale yellow paint, but unfortunately, the new paint had no friendship with the old one, so it was peeling off. The two windows were in good condition, even if one could not open or close them. There were beautiful pink lace curtains in both windows. I could not help admiring these; that's all I saw.

I went back and she wanted to know what I thought of it.

I had nothing to say and so I simply shrugged. She suggested that I go home that evening and think about her offer of staying in. And that is where the story ended, because I never did stay in that room. I had reasons for this: my madam was scared of going down the steps that led from the back door to the pavement outside the girl's room. This meant that whatever happened to me while I was sleeping, I would get no help from her. The room also did not have basic furniture, like a stove or a wardrobe. Nor did my madam care what time I knocked off, which meant I would be part of the family – making tea and serving her friends one way or another until all hours – so I would have no time to study. I did not like the idea, not at all.

Despite all these things, I could not help liking her, because she was somewhat childish; but our friendship did not last long.

The thing started one day when I was making coffee for two of her friends. My madam came in and told me that I should call those two guys 'Baas'!

I was caught off guard this time. 'What! You must be joking!'

These words escaped my lips before I could think of preserving my 'meek front'. I was simply baffled.

What now! My dear madam was at a loss for words. She simply frowned at me. It was hard to believe that these words had come from her exceptionally good girl who always said: 'Yes, Madam' to everything. These guys I had to call 'Baas' were more or less my own age and they started laughing, asking her why I had to call them 'Baas', instead of using their own names. My madam decided we should drop that subject right there.

When everybody was gone and we were left alone, she sent me to a hardware shop nearby to buy some Bostik for her shoes. I was not served when my turn came. When I got back, I told my madam that I would appreciate it if she went to that hardware shop herself if she wanted anything. 'I think they will serve you quickly,' I went on.

'Why?' she asked.

'You are white and it is one of the rules of that hardware to serve whites first, no matter who came first,' I explained.

'Who said that?' she wanted to know.

'Their reaction did.'

'You must forget that you are black and life will not be so difficult,' she said, smiling, and went on before I could even say anything: 'Maybe the way out is to call them "Baas".'

That word again! Things were turning sour for me. This word was becoming a nightmare – or rather a 'daymare', because this all happened during the day.

'I am very sorry if that is the case, because I never call anybody "Baas" whether he is white, red or yellow.'

'I am warning you about your behaviour, my girl. You must be careful about what you say, I'm telling you. South Africa is not a very lovely country for a black person if you do not learn to be respectful.'

I did not ask her what respect meant, but I was soon to find out.

Do you know what happened the following morning? A handful of her friends came round to talk to me.

'About what?' I wanted to know, and the answer I got was, 'Just about life in general.' I felt honoured. I was about to sit and talk to the 'witmense' about life in general!

'How old are you?' asked a tall and good-looking lady.

'I am twenty-one.'

'Where do you stay?' Walk Tall went on.

'In Alexandra,' I said.

'Do you like it there?' This came from a stout guy with a beard; the hair on his head was shiny black and so was his beard, except that it was bushy.

'Yes, I do like it there,' I said.

'How do you find your madam?' Mr Black Beard went on.

'I think she is kind,' I said. (At that moment my madam was visiting the loo.)

'And she thinks you are a good girl,' he smiled.

'I'm glad.' I sort of blushed. I was not very sure where this interrogation was leading.

'She tells me you are interested in journalism,' an elderly lady said, smiling.

'That's true.' I smiled too, not because I felt like smiling but because everyone in the lounge wore a smile.

'How would you feel if you could become a famous journalist?' she went on.

'I don't know.' This called for a good laugh from everyone in the house. Some had to dry their eyes, which were laughing too. Walk Tall was the first to recover, because she did not laugh much. Apparently, she was the kind of person who likes to keep her teeth inside. But her upper lip was short and acted against her. She was calm and collected and her face was expressionless when she asked me this question:

'How do you feel about politics?'

My! The change in the talk about life in general was noticeable, to me in particular …

'Where were you during the 1976 student riots?'

'Would you rather the blacks ruled this country?'

What a lot of questions! I did not know which one to consider first, so I decided that 'I do not know much about politics,' was the right answer.

Then Granny said: 'Do you know anything about Azapo, the Azanian People's Organisation?'

'I know the name of the organisation and that's all,' I replied. I was not pleased at all. We were not talking freely. I was being interrogated and that made me feel bad, because I was not sure how to tackle this and I was getting restless.

'What do you think of Mugabe?' came another bullet from Black Beard. This put everybody on the alert, searching for something in my face.

'I do not understand …' and I meant just that.

'I mean, do you think he is suitable for his position?' explained Black Beard; but I was even more surprised than before.

'Yes, do you think otherwise?'

'Black South Africans think he's great,' said Walk Tall, and they all burst out laughing.

'You people are still going to suffer.' This was directed at me by Granny, who went on to say: 'People who want to help you, people who understand the situation in this country, you call "sell-outs".'

'Yes, this is strange,' said Walk Tall. 'These words "sell-out" and "puppet" are in the air and they are dedicated to the wrong people.'

'You never know how these people see things,' added Black Beard.

My madam had been very quiet. She had been nodding her head in agreement and laughing. Now she decided to say something: 'It is not a matter of seeing things, they are just narrow-minded ...'

Up to now, they had been talking amongst themselves, not to me, but I had a question and so I voiced it: 'Who are these people who are wrongly called sell-outs and puppets?'

I was answered almost immediately by Walk Tall: 'Gatsha Buthelezi, Matanzima ...'

My madam felt she had not finished and so she helped her: '... Mangope.'

'Sebe,' said one man, who had been quiet all along. 'I don't know much about Mphephu, but he is not a bad guy either,' he said. 'Do you also think they are "sell-outs"?'

Before I could say anything, Black Beard came to my aid: 'That is obvious. All girls of her age think so.'

But I still had something to say: 'I happen to have lived in the Transkei, which means that I know more about the conditions there than you do.'

'We do not have to stay there to know how happy the people there are.' That was my madam.

'It is so unfortunate for Matanzima, who does his best for them, that they do not see things his way,' said Walk Tall. 'It is always the case. The black people do not know who their true leaders are.'

'Because they are narrow-minded and their minds are just like this,' said my madam, using her forefingers to show how narrow our minds are. 'All they want is Communism!' she went on.

'That's one thing I hate!' Granny said nervously.

'I don't care what they do with themselves, the moment they bring communists into this country we won't have the smallest worry. We'll just fly back to Europe,' the quiet man said, and I could see that he really did not care.

Walk Tall felt he had not finished his speech and she did the job for him: 'We will leave them crying for our return, just like the people in Mozambique.'

'They are too narrow-minded to see that – just bloody stupid,' my madam put in.

'These people do not know how to live in the first place,' Granny retorted, and this made me feel kind of mischievous, so I said, 'Maybe they will know how to live in the second place.'

Some were amused and some were annoyed at such a foolish comment.

'This girl of yours couldn't live in Ireland nor in Switzerland.'

'She could not afford to go there anyway.'

I sat there looking from speaker to speaker and smiling from time to time. I was not given the chance to say anything and so I pushed my speech in anywhere I felt like it.

'How are things up there?' I asked Black Beard.

'In Ireland? Dear God! Things are just fine there ... I mean everybody respects each other. People are kind and sensible. It's not like this mad country.'

'That's true, people are mad in this country, I'm telling you.' That was Granny. 'I remember at my home, we would leave windows wide open and no one would come in to steal our things,' she went on.

And this made my madam remember something too. 'That's true, look what Shaka and other fools like him did to the people.'

'That's true, and look what Hitler and other fools like him did to the people.' I simply had to say this, even if my opinion was not asked for. The effect was tremendous.

'This girl is mad. By God she is!' the quiet guy shouted, standing up and sitting down again almost immediately.

He was not the quiet guy anymore. I learned later that he was German.

'I'm sorry, I did not mean to be mad.' I had to make my apologies, seeing the cloudy expression on his face.

'My dear girl, if I were you I would thank God that I had lovely clothes like these and a necklace like the one you have on.' (My madam had no overall for me so I was working in my clothes.)

'Her belly is full and there is a roof over her head, that's all that counts,' Granny said. Black Beard felt that I didn't know life yet – that I had never suffered.

'Yes, she cannot believe it when I say I came from a very poor family. I remember once when we lived on potatoes day in and day out for a whole month, when my father fell sick.' That was my madam, her eyes distant. I suppose she could even see herself in those sad days and this made everybody look back into their childhood.

'I also came from a poor family. My cousins would give me their clothes if they did not like them anymore. I never wore anything from the shop.' That was Granny, looking really sad.

'Yesterday, she said she would never call anybody Baas,' my poor madam said helplessly.

'Why do I have to call anybody Baas?' I wanted to know.

'To show respect to those superior to you,' Granny said indignantly.

I laughed lightly and this annoyed everybody in the house.

'These blacks have too much to say, I'm afraid,' Black Beard said.

'You called me for a talk on life in general, not for a lecture on how a black servant should behave.' My tone, as I said this, was very rude and I regretted it. But unfortunately I could not swallow my words.

It was just before 11a.m. when they decided to leave. Surely they had no more interest in me? I was not a good girl at all. I had not even started with my work by that time, so I had to make it snappy, because my madam was going out for lunch. She was very quiet, after telling me that she was disappointed in me. She had thought that I was a good, intelligent girl who knew what was good for her.

I felt really sorry I had said all those things. I wished I had kept quiet, but there's no use in 'if onlys'. I rushed from this corner to that corner, trying to clean the house as quickly as I could, from time to time interrupted by: 'Another cup of coffee, please.'

* * *

One day, my madam sent me to the hardware store to buy something I heard her call 'antrocide'. I had no idea what that was, but all the same I went.

This time, I was the only customer and so they served me without any delay. However, they did not have any 'antrocide'. When I delivered the message to my madam, she decided I should go to all the cafes and the chemist also. They were all puzzled to hear me asking for this so-called 'antrocide'; they all told me that the hardware was the only place that kept it.

This I told my madam, who felt very bad about it. 'This country is mad, you know. In my country antrocide is always available at this time of year.'

She thought all South Africans were stupid and off she went to her ever-welcoming phone. She asked all the people I had gone to why they did not have antrocide. She told each one of them that they should learn to order for the needs of the community.

'What is this nonsense of not having antrocide? You own a hardware shop but you cannot meet the needs of the people.'

She went on like that, feeling very upset indeed.

The following day, she sent me to see if they had any antrocide in stock yet, and we got a negative answer once more.

On the third day, she knew what to do. She phoned some company or other and ordered four sacks of antrocide for delivery. The same afternoon, there was a big truck in front of the house. It was packed with coal sacks and eight or ten of my own people, looking very black indeed. One of the men from the front seat came to tell her that they had brought the coal; this guy, seemingly, was in charge of the group.

She told me to tell the other men who were carrying the four sacks to wait until I had cleared some space in the room underneath. The moment I stepped out of the house, the four guys shot insults at me in Zulu. *'Heyi wena masimb' akho, ulibele ukuvula umsunu endlini thina silinde wena la!'* one said, and another said, *'Kucaban' ukuthi kuyazi lokhu kwesifebe.'* They went on like that.

I was puzzled by their reaction and annoyed too, because I was not the one who had ordered coal from their company, yet they were insulting me. And then you know what they did? They emptied all the coal onto the grass in the corner outside the girl's room, on top of the lawn-mower!

Whose house was that – surely not my madam's? She went wild.

There was a woman friend of hers inside the house and they both dashed out and screamed at the men to stop what they were doing; but the reaction they got was appalling. The men just went on emptying the four bags, then slowly made their way to the gate, unmoved by the angry screams.

I'm sure they understood English, but they did not feel like saying anything about the matter. My madam, beaten, flashed her anger at the man in charge of them and told him to phone his company so she could report him. When he protested, she took the phone herself and did the calling.

The company sent a white guy to come and see 'the damage' as she put it. When the guy came round, he inspected 'the damage' half-heartedly and looked at her in a puzzled way.

'What exactly do you want? Is this not the coal you ordered, delivered right to your door too?' the guy said angrily.

It was my madam's turn to be puzzled.

'Do you want to tell me you think its right to put the antrocide just anywhere – in my lounge, perhaps?'

They were both talking about the same thing, even if they used different names for it. So at last I realised that this anthracite was just coal.

The guy from the company did not have much to say to this. He simply answered, 'Well, it's not in your lounge.' And off he went – just like that.

It was time for me to go home. I was left to wonder how many people my madam phoned to recount the incident to. In the morning, she told me that she had cried all night. She simply could not sleep with such hurt in her heart.

'The guy was terse and rude!' she explained to the company manager, who seemed to be showing some sympathy for her.

I don't know how the conversation between the two of them went, but all I do know is that she still wasn't satisfied, and the next thing she did was to phone the police. My God, she was serious, even saying that she was fighting for her *dignity*! Two young policemen came and she was very friendly to them. She offered them some coffee, but they were there for business and wanted to see the damage. She went outside with them.

They examined the lawn-mower, but there was no damage – only black dust from the coal. The wall, too, was not damaged in any way, except that the soot was still showing here and there.

The policemen said that they were very sorry for what had happened, but they could not do anything for her as there was no evidence of the malicious damage that she had phoned them about.

My madam was not to be that easily beaten, however. She insisted that I make some coffee for them, and they could not but accept the offer. She knew she couldn't keep them any other way, and she still had more to say to them.

'Do you know what these Africans did? They insulted my girl, for no reason at all.'

'What did they say to her?' the policemen wanted to know.

'They said something awful about her womanhood.'

This I had told her when she wanted to know why I was angry.

The policemen wanted to see me and I came. They said, 'Do you want to lay a charge against them? You can do that if you want to.'

This brought a smile to my madam's face and she looked at me hopefully.

'I don't like any involvement with the police, they scare me,' I said.

'So you prefer to forgive those men?'

'Yes Sir,' I said politely.

'What scares you about the police?'

'The guns they carry.'

Both policemen laughed, but my madam was close to tears with anger at my reaction. After they had gone, she came to me and said: 'I am ashamed of you. I was only trying to help you, but you are too foolish to see that. You could even sell me out. You are just like the rest of your people, who are as black-minded as the coal they work with!'

I stayed mute, for fear of upsetting her even more. In fact, I was not very sure about my feelings on the matter. I took my mind back to the happening of the previous day and I could clearly hear the man insulting me. But I felt no anger now. I tried to think why they had reacted that way. I put myself in their position and worked at the problem silently.

It could not be because they were tired from carrying the sacks, because they had only carried them from the truck into the house, which was a short distance. Nor had their rudeness been in response to something I had said to them, for I had not said a word. The conclusion I came to, was that these people have taught themselves to be rude. Why? Because they are forced to do the kind of work they do and because they are always called boys. This has stripped them of their manhood. It has made them feel unsure of themselves, inferior – even to women. To get rid of the humiliation and frustration that dominates them, they spit words that hurt.

At first I was angry, but not anymore. Now, I merely felt sorry for them, because I understood their situation. I only wished that they understood that we, as women, do not look down on them as 'boys'. They are our men. After settling this in my mind, I felt very relieved. My madam and I did not say much to each other for the rest of the day.

The following day, I discovered that the coal was no longer there; and neither were my working shoes, which were kept in the girl's room. The coalmen had come to take their coal back, since my madam didn't want it any more. The shoes, nobody had asked to take. It was a foolish theft, because they were very old.

My battles in domestic work went on. Every day, I was reminded about my colour and every day, I was hurt or angered for one reason or the other. This did not taste good. It is not in my nature to hate anybody. One day, I looked at the calendar and saw that it was again the 29th of the month.

'Tomorrow is the end of the month,' I thought. 'I will get my R40.00 and then I'll get lost, never to be found again in this part of the world.'

I went home that afternoon, wishing a miracle would happen and tomorrow would rush to my rescue. Tomorrow finally came and I waited to be paid.

'I had forgotten it was the end of the month. I'm sorry,' my dear madam said. 'Things will be okay tomorrow. I'll have the money for you then.' And with a contented smile, she dismissed me.

I felt bad to think that I had to wait for yet another tomorrow. What I hated most, was that I did not have a cent for the bus the following day, which meant that I had to borrow a rand from somebody.

I did not even have supper that evening, for I had no spare money at all. Every cent I had had to be kept for the bus.

It was now the first of May and I did not have much to say for myself. I just went on with my work as usual. I could not help thinking that I was not going to be paid for that day's work either; but I went on quietly with it all the same.

Some girls in the neighbourhood asked me if I did not have any problems with my madam when it came to being paid, and I told them that I had not yet been paid for the last month. They laughed at me and said that she was not a lovely person where paying was concerned.

This nagged at me, but I hoped things would be different when it came to me, because I did not wish to have any more problems with her.

She kept asking me why I was not so happy that day and whether something was wrong. I would just keep quiet, or half-heartedly say: 'No, nothing.'

Later that day, she decided I should go and polish the floor at the shop. In short, that was the hardest day ever. While I was still at the shop, I broke a vase and she started telling me that I broke it deliberately, because I had not smiled all day – which showed how lazy I was. I was wondering if smiling was part of my job, but I kept quiet.

It was after 4p.m. when I asked for the money I was owed; she told me to do a big bundle of ironing before I got it.

I was very tired now and I refused to do the ironing, stating that since she would not pay me for that day's work, she must understand that I was not prepared to work for her any longer.

'Dumb girl,' she said, and went inside, leaving me standing there waiting for what was mine.

Her friends were busy chatting happily in the lounge and she went to join them.

It was round about 5p.m. when she finally reappeared

and called me to follow her into the shop. She produced the money, which was only R36.00 and, in explanation, said that I had to pay for the vase I had broken. She said I would pay R2.00 for that, and that the other R2.00 was for everything she had given me, like the two files and the occasional bus fare.

I did not feel too bad about it. All I wanted was to vamoose.

'You must always remember that I will remain the boss and you will remain the slave class. Actually, you will die with a broom in your hand. You will never be anything in your life, because you are black and so is your mind. Blacks will never rule this country, because they have no brains. Do you understand?'

Those were the final parting shots from my dear madam.

'Yes, madam.' I simply had to call her that for the very last time. Then I turned my back, never to show my face again in that part of the world.

Say No

Say No, Black Woman
Say No
When they call your jobless son
a Tsotsi
Say No
Say No, Black Woman

Say No
When they call
Your husband at the age of 60
a boy
Say No
Say No, Black Woman

Say No
When they rape your daughter
in detention and call her
a whore
Say No

Say No, Black Woman
Say No
When they call your white sister
a madam
Say No

Say No, Black Woman
Say No
When they call your white brother
a Baas
Say No

Say No, Black Woman
Say No
When they call a trade unionist
a terrorist
Say No

Say No, Black Woman
Say No
When they give you a back seat
In the liberation wagon
Say No
Yes Black Woman
A big No

My Father

It's such a pity that I stay so far from home. This job of mine ... I'm having a good time with it and I shouldn't be complaining really, since lots of things are going well for me at the moment. But, God knows, I miss home! Maybe this sounds mad for a grown-up woman like me ... but, well, I'm the last born at home, so everybody treats me like a baby; maybe that's what I'm missing. I miss my father especially. I always have such good times with him – not that I go home all that often. The last play that I acted in travelled for six months, and I was exhausted when we finally came back. I knew I didn't need any medicine or pills – all I needed was a lazy week at home.

I took a plane from Johannesburg to Durban; it took me something like two hours in total and by 3.30 in the afternoon, I was home. The whole family was there, gathered together after the big Sunday lunch. That's another thing about being home – a big family get-together! All my married sisters, my brothers-in-law, my brothers and their wives, my nieces and nephews running and falling and crying and laughing ... You know what it's like!

I had my share of grown-up talk and then I had an even bigger share of playing with the kiddies. That's one thing you can bet your last cent on – where there is me there is also noise. I always laugh when I think of how happy my family is when I am home, but God – the noise I make with the children! I suppose they have given up on me ever changing. My father always takes my side though – he says it's because I'm still small myself! He actually buys me sweets when he goes to town, and I enjoy that kind of treatment.

Another thing to mention is that our house is the only one left in the old place; all the other families have been moved to the new township. The authorities have been threatening to move us for ages. My father is adamant – he refuses to move from the house he built with his own hands, where he planted trees, built a strong stone wall for a cattle kraal – everything. The cattle he won't sell, because he loves them and he loves to hear them moo in the mornings. Also, he gets milk from the cows instead of having to buy at the shop. My father loves *amasi* – a dish of *uphutu*, which is free-running mealie porridge and thick sour milk fresh from the calabash. You know, it's things like these that make me love going home – sitting outside under the shade of an *umsalinge* tree and enjoying *amasi* with my father.

And the house itself – it's big, made out of strong, big stones, and it has seven rooms. That's the house we all grew up in; we played a lot on the veranda, made play houses using stones, sand, branches and tins . . . anything we could lay our hands on. Then we'd have to clean the whole yard because we'd made such a mess. But it was fun! There are big trees around the back and then there's the dust road that leads to the shopping centre not very far off. I don't know how many times I came home crying, because I'd lost money in the sand, on my way to the shops. You see, we used to play this game – we'd all sit in the sand on the road and open our legs wide, put down 50 cents or whatever money our parents had sent with us to buy something from the shops. Then we would try to find the money, and whoever found theirs first was the winner. Needless to say, many times the money sank deeper into the sand and earned us a good hiding; I remember that I developed a habit of running off to the Mncadodo River for a swim after those hidings. I don't know why, but it seemed to soothe away the pain. Oh, I still love that home of mine! My father argues that he finds it stupid to move to the townships to a four-roomed box and leave his big house standing there, along with the graves of our grandparents and other members of the family.

Maybe the reason I agree with him is because I live in Johannesburg, where I spend most of the time listening to trucks, buses, motorbikes, fire engines and telephones, breathing polluted air and trying to be on time for this and that . . . When I'm at home, I don't even put my watch on. They go to sleep so early there – I always complain for the first day or two, but then I join them, waking up early each morning to beautiful bird noises. I get excited just thinking about it. I think my father has a point in staying on. But at the same time, I worry a lot about what the authorities are planning. These crazy removals in this country – one can't just stay where one wants and have the kind of house one chooses to have.

It reminds me that I must go down there again before anything happens. My last visit was beautiful as usual; especially memorable, was the day my father and I went to town together. It was a Tuesday, I think. When he suggested the outing to Durban, I looked forward to it very much. I remembered photographs we'd taken on similar trips when I was very young. And the day I cried for hours in town, demanding that he buy me a blue handbag to match my blue dress with goats all over it. I was so proud of that dress! I remember that it had a stiff petticoat.

So we went to town together on that Tuesday, the two of us wearing long corduroy pants and warm jerseys. I think I'm as tall as my father now; no one ever thought, seeing how fat I was as a child, that I'd grow up to be so tall and skinny. The day of our outing was mid-winter, the beginning of July, and it was cold. My mother looked at us from the doorway and she teased that we looked like brothers or close buddies dressed like that. On the train, my father told me about all kinds of changes, updating me on what had happened since my last visit.

The whole thirty minutes to Durban, we talked and laughed softly together. He asked me to remind him about some black shoe polish when we got to town – he'd forgotten to write it down. Another thing he insisted I should not forget when we got back home was to take a photograph of him and his favourite cow; she had a lovely red and white calf.

In town we had a wonderful time, window-shopping, buying this and that. We stopped often to talk to people who knew my father and who were then introduced to his youngest daughter who lives in the City of Gold. We looked at bicycle shops too. My father used to have a bicycle. He always said he felt much safer on that than in a car or a bus. On that subject, my parents hate my habit of coming home by aeroplane. They say I'm running a risk of disappearing high up in the sky and then they will be forced to go up and look for my body amongst the clouds. One of my nephews once asked me how many hours it took from Johannesburg to London by plane. I told him; then he asked me: 'But what do you do if you are too pressed and you want to go to the toilet?' I explained that there are toilets inside the aeroplane. Everyone gasped, imagining that it all fell out on those walking down below.

I always laugh when I think of the young children, shouting when they see a plane flying past: '*Elapren! Elapren!*' Or, '*Banoi*, bring us a little sister!' We used to think that babies came from aeroplanes, that they flew to the hospitals, where our mothers then went to buy their babies.

Anyway, I was telling you about our day in town. We walked up and down the Durban streets and ended up at the beachfront, at some café there. First, we went to see the rickshaws; I still find them fascinating, with their huge feet, bright coloured gear and their amazing headgear with the big horns standing up. Afterwards, we went to have some lunch and drink coffee at the small café. It was quite cold and the sky was overcast, with dark, low clouds. After the coffee, my father suggested we should go and sit on the rocks near the water. The sea was calm and vast. We sat down, took off our shoes and socks and put our feet in the water. It still beats me how water, whether river or sea, always feels warmer to the touch than the cold air outside it.

We stayed like that, with our feet in the water, for what seemed like hours. We talked and talked, all the time looking out to sea. Sometimes, we laughed, but we also spoke about serious things, about me living so far from home and travelling such a lot, and about how I might never know until too late if my parents were sick or already dead.

'Or maybe you will come home one day and find that the white people finally had their way and our house is no more,' my father said. 'What will you do then? Walk around carrying your suitcases and asking people for the new address?'

I didn't answer. I just wished my father hadn't touched on the subject. We sat there for such a long time that we didn't even notice the rain coming. At first, it was just a little rain; then, gradually, the drops grew bigger and bigger.

I looked at my father, waiting for him to say 'let's go', but he didn't. We sat where we were, still talking. I had on a heavy mohair jersey and his jersey was thick too, but that did not protect us from the rain. The rain came down faster and harder, and still we sat there with our feet in the sea water and our shoes filling up with the rain water. My hair at that time was quite long and thick, it was soon wet through. The rain was blowing from behind us and I could feel that I was wet to the skin at the back. I began to find it really funny, you know, as if I were standing in some safe, dry place, watching this old man and his daughter sitting and talking in the rain on a deserted beach in mid-winter! I wanted to laugh! I was freezing and I knew my father was cold too, but since he thought it was alright to just sit there, I decided I was not going to say a word.

And so we sat, while the rain poured down around us, as if it were the most normal thing in the world. Finally, it began to lessen, easing off into a light drizzle that was hardly even rain. My father commented that we hadn't bought his shoe polish yet; with that, he stood up, emptied his shoes of rain water, wrung out his wet socks and put them on. I did the same, and we walked slowly back to the café and ordered two more cups of coffee. I was feeling a little self-conscious walking in, wet as ducks, and sitting down on those nice little chairs. But they let us in and gave us coffee. There were a few people inside; some of them exchanged a glance or two, but then everyone left us alone. We enjoyed our hot coffee, paid, and left them wondering.

In the train, people were actually staring at us. I know we did look a sight – so wet, as if we'd been swimming with our clothes on. Nobody sat next to us. My father looked at the people looking at us and then glanced my way with a smile. I smiled back and sort of chuckled a little. I couldn't help wondering what the people in the train thought of us. And what did they imagine we were smiling about?

'Maybe they think I'm having an affair with him! They must be thinking that he's my sugar-daddy and we've been kissing in the rain somewhere on the outskirts of town …'

I wanted to laugh at myself for even thinking such a thing; I mean, we look so much like father and daughter – our faces are so alike, that even a fool can tell. For the whole journey home, I can't remember us even talking about the rain or about our being wet; no, we just carried on as if we were as dry as everybody else.

Just before sunset that afternoon, my father was milking his favourite cow, the one with the red and white calf. A ray of late afternoon sun was peeping at them through the clouds. I stood there watching, falling in love with the calf myself. Then, I fetched my camera and took a photograph of the three of them – my father, his cow and her calf. I've got the photograph on the wall in my room; I look at it often … and I smile.

I Fell in Love

I fell in love with an old man's prayer
The way he knelt down on one knee
And raised the other to rest his hands on
The way he lifted his face up to the ceiling
And raised his thunderous voice to fill the church

I fell in love with an old man's prayer
The way he took a deep breath to last him long
And praised the God he knew loved and heard him
He praised the God he knew to be the Sun
That shines over our homes whether we are
Rich or poor
The Sun that gives us warmth, light and the very life that is ours

I fell in love with an old man's prayer
The way his whole body swayed steadily
As he praised the God he knew to be the Moon
That shines over our homes to reassure us at night
He praised the God he knew provided
The water we drink and the air we breathe
The stars he knew to be His numerous eyes
That look over each and everyone of us
His kind of God did not sound like a man
With a long white beard and white dress

Then I fell in love with a young girl's voice
The way she sang the Methodist hymns
Like they were written just for her
The way she always stood with her legs apart
Like that was crucial for her to sing
The way she smiled and scratched the back of her neck
Always when she caught me staring at her
I miss the way she searched for my hand
When the old man was about to start his prayer
The two of us never closed our eyes

I fell in love with the old man's prayer
The way he prayed for all of us, young and old
But more for the young and the unborn
The way he seemed to relax and lower his voice
He began to have a conversation with God
And discussed the future of us young people
He wondered if God saw the need for extra strength
For the future did not look very good
He wondered if God realised that some of his people
Had too many problems and some had none at all
He wondered if God had it all planned
That for a part of our stay here on earth
Some people would be poor and others would have everything
Until it was time to change over

I fell in love with the old man's prayer
The way he changed the tone of his voice
The way he wanted God to see sense
He stressed that it was way too long
For the one half to keep bearing their problems
Surely it must be time now for the change-over
Surely God did not want the young to grow up in this darkness
Surely God did not want the unborn to arrive in this cold
Didn't God know that we'd forget how to cook
If we had no food at all
Doesn't God know that we'll forget how to build homes
If we have nowhere to build them

I fell in love with the simplicity of the old man's prayer
Food to eat and a house to make a home

The Crocodile Spirit

The 1960s were certainly times of forced removal in many parts of South Africa. Mr Mkhize's family was no different from any other family that tried to fight to remain in the place of their birth. The government was offering people a few thousand rand as compensation. People were not fooled however; they knew it was not enough. And besides, it was not money they wanted, but to be left alone as a community on the land of their forefathers. The government was not interested in changing its mind, even when the elders sent a delegation to make a plea for their homes not to be demolished.

The bulldozers came early one hot December morning. Everything seemed to happen very quickly, with the drivers deaf to the cries of frightened children, the cackling of hens and sad deep moos from the cattle. Most people were running around frantically, trying to protect their belongings from the monstrous machines each time they made a careless turn near them. The Mkhize family stood with the others, watching as their beautiful homes, vegetable gardens and family graves were flattened to nothing. By midday, the thriving village that had stood so proudly in the beautiful valley near the Ngwenya river, was no more. All that was left of it was rubble and a big cloud of dust that lingered sadly above everything.

There had been quite a few Ngwenya families in that valley. Mr Mkhize had been very good friends with one old man called Mkhulu Ngwenya, or Old Man Ngwenya. He was respected by everyone in the village and whenever people had problems or disputes, they always came to him. He was not the oldest man in the village, nor was he the chief, but somehow, people believed in him and his wisdom.

On that terrible December morning of the bulldozers, Old Man Ngwenya sat on a rock, with both hands supporting his head. His eyes were tightly shut; he could not bear to watch. And he looked so tired that no one dared to speak to him. Everyone seemed to respect that he needed to be left alone with his thoughts and his grief.

The trucks had arrived to load their belongings and carry them away to that strange place out in the wilderness. Someone had already given it a name – Othandweni – which means 'a place of love'. The people were not even given the chance to name the place themselves when they got there. Family names were called one by one through a loudhailer and family after family had to climb on the removal trucks and be driven away. Mr Mkhize's name was called; he was given a number, and he and his family were told to load their possessions onto one of the waiting trucks. His two sons, his little daughter and his wife were already seated on their furniture on the back of the truck. But before he joined them, Mkhize had to go and say goodbye to Old Man Ngwenya.

He found him playing with the dry sand, gently pouring it from one hand to the other, his brow knitted and big tears running down his cheeks and disappearing into his grey beard. He looked very frail. Mkhize mumbled his goodbyes, swallowing hard, feeling that his own tears were near. He was sure that if he were to start crying, he would cry a river, even bigger and more furious than the waters of the Ngwenya river they were about to leave behind them. He touched the old man on the shoulder and hurried away to his waiting family.

As they drove off, Old Man Ngwenya continued to sit on his rock, pouring sand from hand to hand and rocking from side to side. When the bulldozers had flattened the last house and the last family had been driven to the new place, the old man was still sitting there. He had asked to be left behind when his family name was called. His bewildered grandchildren had confusedly waved him goodbye. He said he would later walk to his eldest son's house in the next village. He told them he was just not ready to see the new place. So he was left sitting there, a solitary figure under the scorching summer sun. The big dust cloud had settled and there was a mournful silence over the place. If ever there was a place that deserved to be called Othandweni, it was this one, this beautiful, much-loved valley that had been nurtured by the waters of the Ngwenya River for so many years.

As the sun turned, heading for its home in the western sky, the old man was consumed by a deep longing for his own home. He stood up and walked about in the rubble. His eyes were blinded by tears as he cried like a little boy. He shouted the names of his ancestors, one by one. He wanted them to know that he was still there, that he had not left them behind. But he was also calling on them to assist him to make the right decision. He wanted to be strong for a little while longer. All at once, he stopped dead in his tracks: for a moment, he was sure he'd heard the voice of his late twin brother. He listened hard. But all he could hear now was the sound of running water from the river nearby.

Old man Ngwenya remembered the day his twin brother had been buried, almost twenty years ago. It all came back to him; first, the live twin was put into the coffin, lowered into the grave and then brought back up again, after which the real corpse was put in his place and buried like any other. He remembered that day as if it had happened only that morning. How he wished that his twin brother would suddenly appear now, take him by the hand and lead him to their grave. The old man could no longer tell where his twin brother's grave was, in the wake of those ugly, monstrous bulldozers.

The more he walked around looking for his brother's grave, the more confusing things became to him. The more he longed to climb into the coffin to rest in the cool grave, the hotter the sun seemed to grow. The louder he tried to call his brother's name, the more his head spun and his mouth grew dry. He kept on walking, even though his eyes were not seeing much anymore. He walked slowly and unevenly, like a person in a trance. He was headed straight for the river. He finally stood near the pool where they used to swim as young boys. Then, a strange vision came to him. He thought he saw his late mother. She was sitting on a big flat rock in the river. The strangest thing about this, was that Ngwenya could see right through her belly-flesh, to the twins she was carrying in her stomach. They were very tiny in the womb, but their eyes were open and their little faces looked happy. One looked like his brother and one looked like himself. He was so glad to have found his brother again that he tried to snuggle even closer to him; and as he did so, the Old Man Ngwenya, the real one who was standing at the water's edge, walked forward into the water. He sank and drowned in the deep end of the pool. He did not even make a sound.

More than a month later, Mkhize went back to the old place in the valley near the Ngwenya River. He walked around, feeling like a lost soul at the place of his birth. He had been very saddened by the news of the old man's death. He particularly missed the Old Man Ngwenya. Somehow, he could still feel that old spirit – its presence around him was unmistakable. As he walked, he stumbled over a piece of wood and fell hard. He stood up, brushed himself down and tried to see what it was that he had stumbled over. It was a life-sized wooden crocodile, carved by the old Ngwenya years before as a symbol of his name, Ngwenya, which means 'crocodile'. The carving had always sat on the stoep in front of the old man's hut. Mkhize picked it up and tried to brush the dirt off, but the mud was caked hard. He decided to go down to the river to wash it clean. He washed it with all the care in the world, then dried it in the sun. While he sat there, he felt very close to the old man who had carved it.

Later that evening, at that strange place called Othandweni which was now his home, Mkhize sat with his children and told them stories about the Old Man Ngwenya. He told them of the many disputes Old Man had settled; but mostly, he told them stories about their home in the beautiful valley near the Ngwenya river. Othandweni was a dry and arid place, far from anything. The little creek from where they were supposed to get their water, was dry. They had to wait for a truck to bring them water. It was a sad life that stretched before them in that unfriendly place. Their livestock was suffering too.

Mkhize put the wooden crocodile in front of his own hut. It was special to him and he felt that the spirit of Old Man Ngwenya was with him.

Years later, Mkhize still lived in Othandweni, and he was now an old man himself. On that memorable day of 27th April 1994, Mkhize woke up very early in the morning, ready to go to the nearby school, where he would queue up with all the others waiting to cast their votes. On his way out, he softly patted the wooden crocodile, took up his walking stick and hat, and went on his way, with his little grandson by his side.

Along with many others, Mkhize stood in line in the hot sun outside the polling booth. He chewed his gums and thought about his wife, MaZulu, who had died about a year before. How much he wished right then to see her smile again – she had always smiled like a young girl. While he was queuing, Mkhize thought about somebody else too. He thought about Old Man Ngwenya, and what he would have thought of this great day – the day when many millions of South Africans who had never been able to vote before now patiently waited in line for that great moment. Mkhize seemed to find the strength to bear the hot sun, beating down on him as he stood. It reminded him so much of the day of the bulldozers – that hot and relentless December morning in 1967. He had been so sad then; but today, he had never felt better. For the first time in his life, he would vote!

He entered the polling station and was shown to the

voting booth. Suddenly, he felt strongly the presence of the Old Man. Old Man was laughing and saying to him: 'Go on Mkhize, make your mark! Do it so that bulldozers will never have power over our people's lives again, so that there will be education and hope for our children. What are you waiting for Mkhize? Hurry up and make your mark!'

With a shivering hand, Mkhize held his pencil and made his mark. As he left the booth, he felt so uplifted that he even forgot to use his walking stick! His wife MaZulu, old Mkhulu Ngwenya and many others were there with him in the moment too – united in spirit, and carried away on a huge wave of triumph.

Sometimes When it Rains

Sometimes when it rains
I smile to myself
And think of times when as a child
I'd sit and wonder
Why people needed clothes

Sometimes when it rains
I think of times
When I'd run into the rain
Shouting *'Nkce-nkce mlanjana*
When will I grow up?
I'll grow up tomorrow!'

Sometimes when it rains
I think of times
When I watched goats
Running so fast from the rain
While sheep seemed to enjoy it

Sometimes when it rains
I think of times
When we had to undress
Carry the small bundles of uniforms and books
On our heads
And cross the river after school

Sometimes when it rains
I remember times
When it would rain for hours
And fill our drums
So we didn't have to fetch water
From the river for a day or two

Sometimes when it rains
For many hours without a break
I think of people
Who have nowhere to sleep
No food to eat
And no friends to hold them

Sometimes when it rains
And rains for days without a break
I think of mothers
Who give birth in squatter camps
Under plastic shelters
At the mercy of cold and angry winds

Sometimes when it rains
Rains so hard and hail joins in
As if to add a musical beat
I think of life prisoners
In all the jails of the world
And I wonder if they still love
To see the rainbow at the end of the rain

Sometimes when it rains
With hailstones biting the grass
I can't help thinking
How they look like teeth
Many teeth of smiling friends
Then I wish that everyone else
Had something to smile about

Nokulunga's Wedding

Mount Frere was one of the worst places for a girl to grow up. There, a girl had to marry whoever had enough money for cattle for *lobola*, and that was that. Nokulunga was one of many such victims whose parents wholeheartedly agreed to their victimisation. She became wife to Xolani Mayeza.

By the time she was sixteen years old, Nokulunga was looking her best. Her thighs were long and firm, her breasts stood up so proudly that her younger sister was envious. Her dark, round face was lit up by even white teeth and mischievous-looking big eyes. Many mothers had their eye on her and hoped their sons would act fast, before someone from afar came and snatched her away.

One day, a number of young men came to the river where Nokulunga and her friends used to fetch water. The men were strangers. As the girls came to the river, one of the men jumped very high and cried in a high-pitched voice: *'Hayi, hayi, hayi! Bri-bri mntanam uyagula!'* (which means, 'something must be wrong with you' – i.e. your beauty is unbelievable.)

He came towards the girls and asked for water, walking in the particular style of his region, with his left shoulder pushed down quite low, as if it hurt him, and his right hand carrying two long sticks, which clicked rhythmically as he walked. After drinking, he thanked them and went back to his friends. All the men wore the same kind of trousers, called *imivula*. At the waist, the pants fitted the wearer just right, then they ballooned out from the thigh to the ankle. They were so big at the bottom that Nokulunga thought she could easily make a shirt from each leg of the trousers.

There was nothing new about a few guys passing by and asking for water, but to Nokulunga and her friends, the different clothes they wore and their style of walking were cause for mixed feelings. Some of the girls were very impressed by the strangers, but Nokulunga was not. She was suspicious of them, but decided not to worry about people she didn't even know. She probably would never see them again. The girls lifted their waterpots to their heads and went home.

In late February, the same men were seen again at the river, but now their number had doubled. The sun was very hot, but the strangers were all dressed in heavy overcoats. Nokulunga did not catch sight of them until she and her friends were already near the river. The girls were arguing about something or other, and they did not at first recognise the men as the same ones they had seen at the river two months before. Only when the man who had previously asked them for water came up to them again, did they realise who the strangers were. Nokulunga began to feel uneasy. The stranger drank his water slowly this time, all the while looking at Nokulunga. Then he asked her if he could take her home with him for the night. She was annoyed and did not answer. Filling her waterpot quickly, she balanced it on her head and told the others she had to hurry home. One of her friends followed suit and was ready to go with Nokulunga, when the other men came forward and barred their way.

Things began to happen very fast. They took Nokulunga's pot and broke it on a rock. Many hands wrapped her in big overcoats before she could scream. They slung the bundle that was Nokulunga over their shoulders. The other girls looked on helplessly as the men set off. The strange men chanted a traditional wedding song as they quickly climbed the hillside, while many villagers watched.

Nokulunga twisted round, trying to breathe. She had witnessed girls being taken before. She knew, too, that nobody ever tried to stop such happenings, because they thought the girl's parents were lucky – they would get *lobola*, and their daughter got taken before she could be spoiled. She thought of the many people in the neighbourhood who seemed to love her. They could not love her, if they let strangers take her away without putting up a fight! She felt betrayed and lost. She thought of things she had heard about such marriages. She also knew that her mother wouldn't mind, so long as the man who had taken her had enough cattle.

The journey was long and she was very hot inside the big coats. Her body felt heavy and she was wet with sweat, but the rhythm of her carriers went on and on ...

Her lover, Vuyo, was going back to Germiston to work. He had promised her that he would be away for seven months and then he would be back to marry her. She had been so happy until this moment!

Her carriers were walking down a very steep and uneven path. Soon, she heard people talking and dogs barking. She was put down and the bundle that was her, was unwrapped. A lot of people were gazing at her curiously, wanting to see what the newcomer looked like. She was helped clumsily to her feet and she stood there stupidly in full view of all. She wanted to pee! For a while, no one said anything, they simply stood there looking at her, as if she was a strange species from another planet. The children of the house came in one by one, until the small hut was nearly full. She told them she wanted to go to the toilet and two young women went out with her. Everyone was suspicious that she was trying to get away, so they were all watchful.

After she had relieved herself, she felt better. It was cooler in the evening breeze. She was taken to the hut of Xolani, her husband-to-be, and he came in to join her. They were soon left alone for the night. She sat down calmly, giving no indication that she was intending to sleep at all. Xolani tried to chat with her, but she was silent. So he got undressed and into the big bed made up on the floor. He coughed a few times, then uneasily invited her to join him. Nokulunga sat silently. Xolani was quiet for a while and then he asked her if she was going to sleep that night. No reply. For a long time, she sat there with her big eyes not moving from him. She had to be watchful.

But Nokulunga was tired. She thought he was sleeping, when Xolani suddenly lunged at her and grabbed her arm. His eyes were strange; she could not make out what was in them, anger, hatred or something else. She struggled to free her arm; he suddenly let go and she fell. Quickly she stood up, still watching him. He smiled and moved closer to her. She backed off. It looked like a game, he following her slowly, she backing round and round the little hut. With each round, they moved faster. After a while, Xolani decided he had had enough of the game and he grabbed her again. She was about to scream, when he covered her mouth. She realised it was foolish to scream, it would only summon helpers to him. She still stood a chance if they were alone.

He was struggling to undress her when Nokulunga went for his arm. She dug her teeth deep and tore a piece of flesh out. She spat. His arm went limp, he groaned and sat, gritting his teeth and holding his arm. Nokulunga sat too, breathing heavily and hardly believing what she had just done. Her big eyes grew even bigger with apprehension, knowing he was going to get very rough. Xolani stood up quickly, cursing under his breath and kicked her as hard as he could. She whined with pain but did not stand up to defend herself. Blood was dripping from Xolani's arm and he softly ordered her to tear a piece of sheet to tie above the bite. She tied his arm and wiped the blood from the floor. Xolani got under the bed covers in silence. Nokulunga pulled her clothes together but she didn't dare to fall asleep. Whether Xolani slept, only he himself could say. But the pain in his arm surely didn't make it easy.

It became day again. Xolani left the room and Nokulunga was given something to eat and then locked up. She had swallowed a bit of her food, when suddenly she heard many men talking outside. They entered the house next door, only to leave again minutes later, continuing their loud and excited talk. Then they departed out of range. Nokulunga gave up listening and ate the soft porridge that had been brought to her.

The men sat down next to the big cattle-kraal. Xolani was there with his father, Malunga, and his eldest brother, Diniso. The rest were uncles and other members of the family. They drank their beer slowly. They were all very angry with Xolani. Malunga was too angry to think straight. He looked at his son with contempt and kept balling his hands into fists. No one said anything. They stole glances at Malunga and their eyes went back to stare at the ground. Xolani shifted uneasily. He was holding his hurt arm carefully. His uncle had tended to it, but the pain was still there. His father sucked at his pipe, knocked it out on a piece of wood next to him, then spat between his teeth. The saliva jumped a long way into the kraal and they all watched it.

'Xolani!' Malunga called his son, softly, but angrily.

'Bawo,' Xolani replied, without looking up.

'What are you trying to tell us? Are you telling us that you spent all night with that girl and failed to sleep with her?'

'Father, I … I …'

'Yes, you failed to be a man with that girl in that hut! That is the kind of man you have grown into, unable to sleep with a woman the way a man should.'

Silence followed. No one dared to look at Malunga. He busied himself, refilling his pipe as if he were alone. After lighting it, he looked at the other men.

'Diniso, are you listening with me to what your brother is telling us? Tell us more Xolani, what else did she do to you, my little boy? Did she kick you in the chest too? Tell me, father's little son?' He laughed harshly.

An old man interrupted: 'Mocking and laughing at the fool will not solve our problem. So please, everyone think of the next step from here. The Mjakuja people are looking for their daughter. Something must be done fast.' He was out of breath when he finished. The old man was Malunga's father from another house. It would be necessary to send a message to Nokulunga's family, to let them know her whereabouts. Thirteen head of cattle and a well-groomed horse were waiting to be brought to the family of the abducted girl, together with a goat that served as *imvulamlomo* – 'the mouth opener'.

The sun was setting now and Nokulunga stood for quite a while behind the house, staring into the light of the orange and red ball that was going down in an unknown country behind the mountain. By the time the orange and purple colours faded from the Western skies, she was still looking at the same spot, but her eyes were seeing her future, which seemed to be getting hazier every minute, just like the night falling around her. She had not managed to escape that day. She felt weak and miserable. A group of boys had sat all day on the nearby hill, watching her so that she didn't try running away. She knew she was there to stay.

She had no idea how long she stood there behind the hut. She only came to herself again when she heard a little girl laughing next to her. The child told her that the people had gone out to look for her because they all thought that she had managed to get away while the boys were playing. She went back into the house. Her mother-in-law and the other women also laughed when the little girl said she'd found Nokulunga standing behind the hut. More boys were sent to tell the pursuers that Nokulunga was safely at home. She hated the long dress and the head tie she had been given to wear; they were too big for her and the material still had hard starch on it. It made an irritating sound when she walked, like that made by a horse eating grass. The people who had gone out looking for her came back, laughing and teasing each other about how stupid they had been to run so fast without first checking behind the house.

Nokulunga was trembling as it grew darker. She knew things would not be as easy as they had been the night before. She knew the family would take further steps, although she didn't know exactly what would happen. She was in her husband's room, waiting for him to come in. The hut suddenly looked and felt so small; she felt it move to enclose her in a painful death. She held her arms across her chest, gripping her shoulders so tightly that they ached. The door opened and a number of men of her husband's age came in quietly. They closed the door behind them. Some of them were a little embarrassed, or so they seemed to her. She watched Xolani undress as if he did not want to. His arm did not look any better as he stood there in the dim light of the kerosene lamp. She broke into tears. The men held her tightly and undressed her. Her face was wet from sweat and tears, and most of all, she felt the urge to go to the toilet. The men laughed at her as she pleaded to go. One of the men teased her especially and told her to lie on the bed. When Nokulunga saw the expression on Xolani's face, she cried uncontrollably. He stood there with eyes wide open, as if he were in the country of dreams, and he looked like a lost and helpless little boy. Was this the man she should respect as a husband? How was he ever to defend her against anything or anyone?

Hands pulled her down. Her streaming eyes could not see which man it was who shouted at her that she should lie like a woman. She wiped her eyes and saw Xolani approaching her. She jumped up and pushed him away, grabbing her clothes, but the group of men was onto her like a mob in no time at all. They roughly pulled her back onto the bed and Xolani was placed on top of her. Each of her legs was pulled apart by a man. Other men held her arms. Xolani's friends were cheering and clapping their hands while he jumped high, now enjoying the rape. One man joked that he had had enough of holding the leg and wanted a share of his work. Things were said too about her bloody thighs, amidst roars of laughter, before she fainted.

'The bride is ours
The bride is ours
Mother will never go to sleep
without food
without food.

The bride is ours
The bride is ours
Father will never need for beer
will never need for beer . . .'

The young men were sitting near the kraal. Girls giggled as they sang and performed Xhosa dances. Soon, they would be expected to dance at Xolani's wedding. They were trying out new hairstyles so that each would look her best. The young men, too, were worried about how they would look. Some of them were hoping for new relationships with the girls of Gudlintaba. That place was known for its good-looking girls with their beautiful voices. Others saw that existing relationships might well break up as a result of that wedding. Everyone carried that day of celebration in their own hands; it was up to them whether fighting or laughter ended the day.

The women at Nokulunga's home were also very busy. They prepared beer and took turns going to the river for water, happy and lightfooted as they walked. Time and again, a woman would run from hut to hut, calling at the top of her voice, ululating joyfully:

'Lilili ... lili ... lili ... liiiiiii!
To give birth is to stretch your bones!
What do you say, woman who never gave birth?'

Nokulunga spent most of the time inside the house, with one of her friends and her mother's sisters tending to her face. They had made a concoction of eggs and tree bark, mixed with other things. All day long, Nokulunga's face was encrusted with thick liquids supposed to be good for her wedding-day complexion. Time and again, her mother's sister would sit her down and tell her how to behave now that she was a woman. How she hated the subject! She wished the days would simply pass without her noticing them.

'Ingwe iyawavula amathambo 'mqolo –
The leopard opens up the back bones'

Nokulunga heard girls happily singing outside. She hated the bloody song. The only thing they all cared about was the food they were going to have on that day – the day she wished would never come. Many times, she would find herself just sitting there with her masked face, looking out of the tiny window. She hated Xolani and his name. She felt that he was given that name because he would always do things to inconvenience other people, then he would keep on apologising and explaining; Xolani means – 'please forgive'.

The dreaded day came. Nokulunga walked slowly by Xolani's side. All around her, people were singing and laughing and ululating and clapping their hands. She did not smile, for when she tried, tears came rolling down her cheeks to make her ashamed. For Xolani, it was the day of his life. Such a beautiful wife and such a big wedding! He was smiling at her and squeezing her hand; that was the moment when Nokulunga saw Vuyo. He must have left everything and rushed back home as soon as he heard that his own love had been stolen from him. Vuyo was looking at Xolani with loathing, his fists very tight and his lips pressed together in a hard line. Nokulunga pulled her hand from Xolani's and took a few steps towards Vuyo. She began to cry, wanting so much for him to come and take her hand and run away with her, to some place very far from here; leaving all these mad-happy people to enjoy their meat and beer and celebration without her. Xolani noticed her tears and tried to comfort her. A lot of people saw this; they stood watching, some sympathising, others wondering …

Months passed. Nokulunga was sitting by the fire. In her arms was a five-day-old baby boy, sleeping so peacefully that she smiled at him. Her father-in-law had named the child Vuyo. How thankful she had been for that! She would always remember her Vuyo of old, whom she had loved. She had by now accepted that Xolani was her lifetime partner and that there was nothing she could do about it. Once, she saw Vuyo in town and they had briefly kissed. It had been clear to both of them, however, that since Nokulunga was already pregnant, she was indeed Xolani's wife. Vuyo knew he would have to pay a lot of cattle if he took Nokulunga with her unborn baby. There was truly nothing to be done.

We Are at War

Women of my country
Young and old
Black and white
We are at war
The winds are blowing against us
Laws are ruling against us
We are at war
But do not despair
We are the winning type
Let us fight on
Forward ever
Backward never

Women of my country
Mothers and daughters
Workers and wives
We are at war
Customs are set against us
Religions are set against us
We are at war
But do not despair
We are bound to win
Let us fight on
Forward ever
Backward never

Women of my country
We are at war
Mother Africa's beloved daughters
Do you see what I see?
Forces of exploitation
Degrade Mother Africa
As well as us, her daughters
Her motherly smile is often ridiculed
She has seen her children being sold
Her chains of slavery are centuries old
There is no time for us to cry now
She has cried rivers of tears
What is it that flows down River Nile
If not her tears
What is it that flows down River Congo
If not her tears
What is it that flows down River Zambezi
If not her tears
What is it that flows down River Limpopo
If not her tears
What is it that flows down River Thukela
If not her tears
And what is it then that flows down River Kei
If not Mother Africa's tears

Women of Egypt and Libya
Drink her tears from River Nile
And you will gain courage and bravery
Women of Congo and Liberia
Drink her tears from River Congo
You will shed inferiority
Women of Zambia and Zimbabwe
Drink her tears from River Zambezi
You will gain understanding

Women of Namibia and South Africa
Drink her tears from River Limpopo
You shall see liberation
We the chained women of Africa
We are bound to win
Let us fight on
Forward ever
Backward never

Dumisani

'My son is eleven years old and he is a Standard One pupil at a lower primary school near here. He was arrested on 11th July on his way home from school. It was raining on that day, it was about two in the afternoon and many children were walking home. My son ran away from the rain and went for shelter in an old shack by the road. At the same time, a street or two from where he was sheltering, the older students were stoning cars and buses. I am told that it started long before the rain began to fall, and the police were now chasing the children in all directions. One policeman jumped the fence into the yard where this shack was. He looked around; all those boys that he was chasing had gone – you know how it is in Alexandra, the houses are so close together and there are many double-ups – small paths that run through the houses into the next street ... only people who stay there would know their way around. The police have a hard time. So this one policeman was looking around and he couldn't see where the boys had disappeared to, and then he saw this small boy in the shack. He didn't ask questions, he just said, "Let's go," and away he took him.

'I didn't know what had happened to my son. It was getting late and he was nowhere to be seen. At first, I was angry that he was not home yet; you see, Dumisani knew that he had to come straight home so that we could have somebody to help with this or that in the house. We might need to send him to the shops for something, or Dumisani would be the one who helped me bring the coal in for the stove, or sometimes, he would hold the baby for me if it cried and I was busy. He is generally a very helpful child. It got to six o'clock, then seven went by, and then I began to panic. It was winter, so it got dark very quickly. I just could not think what could have happened to him. I decided to go out and look for him. I was going to ask the husband of the woman across the road to drive around with me so that we could try and find my child. We were going to look around the township, ask some friends of his, our relatives – anybody who could help. But somehow, I had this feeling that we would end up at the police station, even though I could not think why he would be there. I was almost ready to go, when there was a loud knock at the door – only one kind of fist makes that kind of sound, and for sure, it was the police. They came in, one black policeman and many white policemen. The black one was holding Dumisani by the hand and he came in with him.

'Some of the white police stood outside on the veranda and quite a big group of them came into the house – you can see how small this room is. They all stood here and looked around the room, smelling the food – one of them commented that the spinach smelled nice. The black policeman stood in front of me and asked me if the boy was my son. I said yes. He asked Dumisani if I was his mother and he said yes. He was a tall, dark man with a hard look on his face, you could see that he was a cruel person, they are all like that. He spoke in Zulu, saying to me: "We have arrested your son." I asked: "Why, what has he done?" "He was stoning cars and buses this afternoon, that is why we have arrested him." I just didn't know what to say. I looked at my child standing there, with the policeman not letting go of his hand. I just couldn't believe he had done such things. Then they said I must ask him myself. He was not looking at me and my heart went out to him; he is such a quiet child. He tried to explain a little, but it was like he had lost his speech. The policemen told me to come along to the police station, they said I was wasting their time. I put on my shoes and raincoat and followed them out. They lead us out to a hippo! I had never thought I'd have to climb into a hippo in my whole life. I didn't even know where to step to climb in. I asked one of the policemen to help me up. My son was already up. Still, he was not allowed to sit next to me. Poor child; even if he was really guilty, why come in this mad machine, why all these mad men for one defenceless child? I couldn't think of anything else the whole journey up to the police station, I just thought of being raped. Most of the white policemen were very young, but I knew they could do anything, they could rape me! We've heard so many stories of young girls being raped by the police and soldiers. We fear them.

'The inside of the hippo looked very weird. The seats were like little plastic toilet seats in a long row. I don't know how many there were because it was dark, but there seemed to be a lot on each side. I could not see out. I sat there wishing we would get there quickly, before they could do anything to us. My child was sitting opposite me with these big men on either side of him. Tears were rolling down his face; he looked bewildered to me. He couldn't really make out what was happening to him with all these white men around him. A child is a child; you could see that he did not know what to do. What worried me most was the cold. It was so very cold and he did not have much on. He was in his school khaki shorts, a thin polo neck under his khaki shirt, and that was all. He had his socks and shoes on, but that was hardly warm enough for the kind of cold that the rain had brought, especially now that it was night. He had no books with him. He told me he had left them at school because of the rain ... He hardly said anything really.

'We arrived at the police station and they showed me a statement which they said Dumisani had written. Probably, they were beating him when he wrote it; they wanted him to agree that he was stoning buses and cars and that that was the reason why he went to hide in the shack. My God, it was all there, in his scribbly little child's handwriting. I was confused by the whole thing. I just prayed. I said, "Please God, let them warn him and let him come home with me." He is still so small, I never really thought it was all that serious. They then said to me that I must go and the child would remain. I started to cry. Dumisani was looking at me and crying too, but I was not allowed to speak to him privately. They made him sit on this long bench and I had to stand by the desk where the policeman was reading the statement. There were many other policemen in this room or office. I stood still, even when they had said I must go home. They asked me what the matter was. I said I still did not understand what they were saying to me. They asked if I didn't believe that my child had been stoning people's cars. I asked the policeman if he had seen him do it. He said he hadn't, he only found him standing inside the shack, but he knew he was part of that group. I asked him how it was that the boy didn't get wet when it was raining so hard, because everyone else, including the policeman who had arrested him, had been wet. He did not answer me. Then another policeman said that they had seen him on June 16th at the 1976 commemoration service at Nobuhle Hall. I asked them why they had not arrested him then, if they had picked him out among those many, many people. I could not believe the lies from these people! Dumisani had been at Thembisa on that day. I remember it well. I had sent him with Lindiwe, an older girl, because he cannot go to Thembisa on his own. But they insisted that he was there, in Soweto, and that they'd seen him. I was too confused to argue anymore. So I left my son there, and one of the policemen drove me home.

'That night, I hardly slept a wink. How could I sleep, knowing that my child was left alone there with those madmen; thinking how cold he must be in the cell they'd put him in, while I was in my warm bed, in a house kept snug and warm by the heat of the coal stove. The next morning, I went with my cousin to the police station, as they had told me to do. At 8a.m., we arrived at the gate and found this *mantshingilane* – security guard – who let us in; but he first wanted to know what I had in my bag. I told him I'd brought a warm track suit for my son to change into. He refused to let me in with it. He said he'd keep it until a policeman from inside told him it was fine to let it through. That sounded very strange to me, but I couldn't do anything about it. The only thing you are allowed to take in with you is your small handbag with the money. When we went in, we found Dumisani already seated on the bench, as before, with the same black policeman who'd come to the house with him. We sat down and greeted him. He looked so scared and tired, as if he hadn't moved from that bench since the night before. We sat there for a long time; nobody paid any attention to us. We couldn't even make conversation, because the policemen were there all the time. So we just sat.

'We'd been sitting like that for some time when a big boy came in and sat down next to us. He had come from outside. He greeted us and then asked if Dumisani was my son. I said yes and then he asked what he was doing there. The black policeman told him that he'd been arrested. The boy was shocked and asked why. They told him that Dumisani had stoned buses and that he had destroyed somebody's Mercedes Benz. Then they told him that he shouldn't ask too many questions, because when these children were beating up women, stoning cars and destroying somebody's Mercedes Benz, he hadn't done anything to stop them; instead, he went to the movies. It turned out that this young man belonged to Cosas – the Congress of South African Students, or Ayco, which was the Alexandra Youth Congress. The policemen told him that if he was their leader, he should have stopped them from doing wrong, instead of running off to the movies. He just kept quiet. I don't know, but I think he was looking for some colleagues of his who had been taken in too.

'It was after ten in the morning when they told us to follow one of the policemen outside. They didn't tell us where we were going, but I assumed it was to court. They had told me when I asked them that I was not allowed to change Dumisani's clothes. I kept quiet after that. My cousin and I were put into the back of the van and my son went in front with them. In all this time, I had not even touched my son. We drove off to Randburg to see the Commissioner of Oaths, so the boy could swear in front of him that he had done all those things he had written in his statement. Only I was allowed in; my cousin was told to remain outside. I entered and sat down. They took my son forward to stand in front of this huge Afrikaans man who was a Commissioner of Oaths. They brought in another big man, a black man, to translate, because the Commissioner spoke only Afrikaans. They made Dumisane rewrite what he had written in his statement at the police station. He asked them one question, he said: "If I tell you the honest truth, will you let me go home with my mother today? I am very cold." And they said, "Ja, tell us the truth and we'll let you go." So he told them the truth, how he hid in the shack because of the rain, and that was all. And how that other statement about stoning buses and a Mercedes Benz only happened because the police were hitting him and he was afraid. I knew that they would never let him go. They made him sign his statement. They put a pen in his hand and he signed, slowly and carefully. What a strange feeling it was for me to sit there and watch him! Then they told him to raise his hand up like this and make an oath. An oath for all those lies, and this Commissioner man couldn't tell which was the truth! As for me, they would not let me say anything, they would not let me stand up for my child, they would not let me. Anyway, they signed and stamped their papers full of lies and they drove us back. Again, Dumisani sat in front with them. And it was still very cold. I'll never forget that day. To think that we, who were warmly dressed, were so cold ... how much more so must he have been, who had no warm clothes at all ...

'Well, when we got to the police station I gave him some food which I'd brought for him. It was in the afternoon now; you know these people take their time. We sat there with Dumisani holding the food, not eating. I was crying. I didn't know what to do. My child was shivering and he looked down at the ground. Then they told us to go home; the child, they'd lock him up. I was crying and Dumisani was crying too. My cousin was getting impatient with me, she said to me, "You are so busy crying, you don't even ask how long they'll keep him in." I wiped my tears and asked them, but they did not answer my question, they just told me that he would be going to Court 15. My cousin said, "Ask them when he is going to that Court 15!" They said, on Monday. But that was not enough information, she demanded to know where the Court was. The policeman looked at her grudgingly, as if to say she was asking too many questions. He told us it was Court 15 in West Street, in a big courthouse there. I was lucky to have my cousin with me. My own mind was not working properly. Then I asked my child why he was not eating and he said he couldn't eat, he said that the policeman had kicked him on the jaw and his big tooth on the side had come off and the inside of his mouth was peeling. He said it in front of this policeman; the man denied it. He said he had only beaten Dumisani hard on the buttocks. When I asked if I could bring my son some food again, they refused. They said they had food for him. I left him there. When I went to visit again on Saturday, they wouldn't let me see him. On Sunday, they again refused; they only told me that he was not eating. I asked to see him so that I could ask him myself; they refused.

'So on Monday, we went to court. I was going to court for the very first time in my life. The whole place gave me shivers. I don't have a husband, so I went with my cousin's brother. I needed to go with a man; my knees were shaking, but I tried not to cry. I had warm clothes for Dumisani, just in case they agreed to let him change, but of course they didn't. He came in and stood there; you should have seen him, you wouldn't have thought he was my child the way that he was so dirty and hungry-looking! They didn't even let him speak one word, but remanded the case. Then I stood up and asked that man, that magistrate, I asked him to let me take my child home. I asked for bail, but no, they didn't want to hear.

'Then we got a lawyer. The next Monday, we went to court again, but there was no trial. They had transferred Dumisani to John Vorster Square Prison without telling us. It was so frustrating. On Tuesday, the case went on in West Street and Dumisani told them the same story, that he hadn't done any of those things he was accused of doing. He looked like he had lost so much weight, and his hair had grown and was unkempt. And the case – yo! It took the whole day. They were asking questions and the lawyer was talking for us. Some things I didn't understand – you know the language they use in courts ... When they came to me, they asked if he was my son and they asked if he went to school. I said, yes; even a fool could see his dirty uniform, but they still asked. They asked if he was a naughty child. I said no, he was not naughty, he came straight home after school and was very helpful around the house. I told them that I had a hard time now that he was away. Also, I told them that they must give him bail, because he had to go to school. The lawyer tried his best for us. And the principal also wrote a letter – we gave it to the lawyer – to say Dumisani was a good child. They still refused bail. They said he would skip the country and go to Botswana like many others who had been given bail. Or, if he didn't skip, then the Cosas students would burn him, along with the house at night, because they'd think he was a sell out. They said it was in the boy's interests and safety that they were keeping him inside.

'I was very worried about his safety with them. Every time I saw him, something was wrong with him, they'd hurt him more; this time, the bridge of his nose was swollen and bruised. And how can an eleven-year-old child go to Botswana alone, when he can hardly even go to Thembisa on his own? He doesn't even know where it is on the map. One of the policemen went to the principal and asked what kind of child Dumisani was. He said that he was a quiet boy, and very clever. He told the policeman that they should bring him back so he could write his test with the others. The policeman said, but how come his mother says he is such a naughty boy who won't listen? The principal was confused. So you see how they lie all the time.

'Our lawyer fought very hard to get him bail. It took a very long time, but finally the case was taken to the Supreme Court, and there they gave him bail. He stayed with the lawyer for a few days, then he came back. So he's trying to relax now. But he has bad dreams and screams at night. And he forgets things. I send him to the shops to buy one litre of paraffin and he comes back with a litre of coke. His gums are still not right. I'm very worried about him, but I think he will be all right in time. He has been through so much for his age. I think it will take him a long time before he forgets – if he ever forgets ...'

* * *

We had finished our interview and Mrs Goduka insisted that I stay for supper. While she was getting the plates and other things ready, her seven-month-old baby woke up and started crying. She went and changed the nappy. Then she started playing with the child, throwing it into the air, with the baby squealing happily each time she caught it and threw it into the air again. I was watching them against the candle light, and laughing with them.

Then she said: 'Laugh my baby, laugh while you still can. You don't know what a world you are growing up into. Tomorrow, they'll be coming for you.' I think I saw tears in her eyes, but it was hard to be sure; she was laughing and kissing the little baby's bum.

Sitting Alone Thinking

Lately I have more than once
Found myself sitting alone, thinking
Not that I have such a lot of time
Just to sit and think –
I'm a busy woman with a heavy schedule
I have to try and keep up
With the fast world around me

But then somehow it happens
Right in the middle of all the hustle and bustle
Everything just stops
And I find myself sitting alone, thinking
Would Mr President be a better man
If he had a womb and breasts full of milk?
Would he be impressed by the number of children jailed
All in the name of peace, law and order
If he had just one ten-year-old in jail
Would the smell of tear-gas and bloody bullet wounds
Be so appetising as to bring
That familiar smile to the President's face
If he had a womb and breasts full of milk?

All these visions come up to me
When I'm sitting alone thinking
Thinking of my very best friend
As she sits in a jail cell
Longing for her little baby
Her painful breasts full of milk

It's Quiet Now

Everyone seems to be going to bed now. The rain is coming down in a steady downpour and I don't think it's going to stop for a long time. Normally, I would be joining the others, going to bed while it's still raining, so that I can enjoy the sound of it while I wait for sleep to come and take me. But tonight is different. I don't even feel like playing any soft music either. I just want to stand here at the window and watch what can be seen of the rain coming down in the dark.

The news in the papers is always the same: people's houses petrol-bombed, youths and activists arrested, suspected informers necklaced, police shootings … it only varies from place to place. It's been like this for … I don't know how long It's really depressing. Today, I didn't even have to buy a paper to know what's been going on; things have been happening here since late this morning.

For a while now, the Putco buses have not been going into the townships; but last week, they started coming into our township again. The newspapers said that the local Residents' Association had asked the authorities to bring back the buses, but members of the Association know nothing about it. Most old people seemed quite relieved that the buses were back, but they knew it wouldn't last. Company delivery vans have not been coming in either; the students have burnt so many of them in the past few months. The house of the local 'Mayor' was also burnt down. It was one o'clock in the morning when we were woken up by two loud explosions, one after the other, and soon the house was eaten up by hungry flames. The 'Mayor' and his family just made it out of the house in time, running for their lives. Everything was burnt to ashes by the time the police and the fire-engines arrived. When I saw what was left of his house, I remembered what the 'Mayor' had said a few weeks back in a Residents' meeting: 'You seem to forget that I am as black as you are, and I suffer just like you do under the apartheid laws of this country.' The grumbling of the audience showed that nobody believed him.

A lot of things have been happening here; I just can't keep track. Young children who hardly understand what's really going on are also shouting the slogan '*Siyayinyova*,' which simply means 'We will destroy or disrupt.'

Nobody was expecting anything out of the ordinary today, even though there were more policemen than usual; there have been police driving up and down our streets for quite a while now. We carry on with our work and sort of pretend they are not there.

I was carrying on with my work as well, when I suddenly heard singing. I ran to the window and there, at a school in Eighth Avenue, these children – you know I can still see them as if there's a photograph in my mind – they poured out of their classes into the streets, where the police were. They were shouting '*Siyayinyova!*' at the tops of their little voices. They picked up rocks and bricks and started attacking buses, company delivery vans and police cars. When the police started chasing them, they ran through double-ups, the small paths that cut through people's houses. I stood transfixed at the window. There was running everywhere, just school uniforms all over the township, and shouting and chanting and screaming and burning of houses – both policemen's and councillors'.

The company vans were burnt in front of the house right opposite us. The fire jumped and caught the house as well. Black smoke was pouring from everywhere, from the house and the car, and the cars in the next street and the next ... Soon the streets were lost in dust and smoke.

Clouds from earth began to meet clouds from the sky. We suddenly heard '*ghwara! ghwara!*' Lightning and thunder. Louder than any bomb or gun. Poor soldiers, their guns came down as the rain began to fall – *whhhaaaaa* ... Maybe the rain came to clean up the mess.

People started coming back from work. It kept on raining and no one even ran for cover. They walked in the rain as if everything was just as they had left it. Some had heard the news at work, and others could see that a lot had happened. But they walked home as usual and got on with their suppers. I didn't have any appetite at supper. I'm wondering if it's safe to go to sleep now. There is only a light drizzle coming down, and all seems quiet in the night.

The Dancer

Mama,
they tell me you were a dancer
they tell me you had long
beautiful legs to carry your graceful body
they tell me you were a dancer

Mama,
they tell me you sang beautiful solos
they tell me you closed your eyes
always when the feeling of the song
was right, and lifted your face up to the sky
they tell me you were an enchanting dancer

Mama,
they tell me you were always so gentle
they talk of a willow tree
swaying lovingly over clear running water
in early Spring when they talk of you
they tell me you were a slow dancer

Mama,
they tell me you were a wedding dancer
they tell me you smiled and closed your eyes
your arms curving outward just a little
and your feet shuffling in the sand;
tshi tshi tshitshitshitha, tshitshi tshitshitshitha
O hee! How I wish I was there to see you
they tell me you were a pleasure to watch

Mama,
they tell me I am a dancer too
but I don't know ...
I don't know for sure what a wedding dancer is
there are no more weddings
but many, many funerals
where we sing and dance
running fast with the coffin
of a would-be bride or a would-be groom
strange smiles have replaced our tears
our eyes are full of vengeance, Mama

Dear, dear Mama,
they tell me I am a funeral dancer

Fly, Hat, Fly!

Robben Island must be one of the most famous islands in the world. It has been used for various purposes over the centuries. Once, it was a leper colony, then it became a maximum security prison for men who opposed colonial domination. Makhanda kaNxele, a Xhosa leader, was one of the very first known political prisoners. Leader of the PAC (or Pan-Africanist Congress), Robert Sobukhwe, was also sent to the island prison by the Nationalist government. Many more like him followed; but the most famous of them all was our first black President, Nelson Mandela.

This history was not the kind we were taught in our schools, but we knew it. Many of our own fathers, husbands, sons, brothers and uncles had been banished to that place for life. Some of those men are now holding key positions in the government. Some are doing very well indeed; others are living in obscurity and maybe even worse rural poverty than they remember from the days of their youth.

Just over a thousand ex-Robben Island prisoners came to a reunion organised by a Cape Town-based organisation called Peace Visions. It was on the weekend of 10th February 1995, about nine months after the first democratic elections in South Africa. Many of these men had never thought that they would ever meet again after they had been freed from prison. They had formed strong bonds in jail. Although they came from diverse organisations like the ANC, PAC, Black Consciousness Movement and AZAPO, they had learned a lot from one another and had lived as brothers, fighting for the same cause.

The Robben Island reunion on February 10th was a bright sunshiny day in Cape Town. The ex-prisoners came from all over South Africa in their hundreds, to board the rented boat, *The Oceano*. It could hold more than a thousand people.

Robben Island had been a men's only prison and so there were very few women who came to the reunion; I was one of them. Some of the faces were easy to recognise, but others were quite unfamiliar. The emotions were varied. Some people were ecstatic at seeing their comrades again, others looked pensive and seemed to be lost in their own thoughts, and yet others were talking quietly to one another, only to be startled by a call of recognition from someone they had not seen in years.

With all of this going on, I felt honoured and humbled to be in the presence of these freedom fighters. I was all eyes and ears, catching all kinds of facial expressions and bits of conversations. I felt saddened as I watched comrades learning of a dear friend's death and other sad news. But what I remember most about the day, was an incident which only lasted for maybe a minute or two.

I was walking from one part of the boat to another. I climbed the stairs slowly, as there was a relatively old man in front of me, and I was in no hurry anyway. As the man reached the top step, he stood still and looked out to sea. Then, taking off his hat, he turned to me, saying: 'Look, my child, this hat is apartheid.' With this, he squashed the hat into a ball and threw it with all his energy into the sea. 'See, I have thrown away apartheid! I never want to set my eyes on it again.' I watched his hat, which regained some of its shape and then sailed off away from us as we moved slowly towards Robben Island. I did not know what to say. My eyes came back and met those of the grey-haired man, who looked so happy and yet so sad. He seemed quite strong for his age. We smiled at each other for a brief moment. The old man turned back to the hat again. I heard him say, this time to himself: 'Fly, hat, fly!'

A few minutes later, he had moved on to talk to some men whom he obviously knew from prison. I found myself a place to stand where I could still see the hat as it grew smaller and smaller in the distance. I wondered why he had chosen to share his symbolic act with me, rather than one of his comrades. My mind was suddenly crowded by visions of the many men who had been humiliated in front of their children and wives, men who had had to take off their hats in front of an employer or some other official. They had to take off that hat, squash it and swallow all sorts of insults and degradation. This hat brought back so many painful memories. And it certainly was one of the symbols of apartheid. The old man had thrown away something that symbolised oppression for him. Did this mean that each and every South African had to quietly find his or her own symbol to throw away in their own individual way? I walked away, feeling very thoughtful, wondering what I would choose as my own 'hat' to throw overboard and tell to 'Fly, hat, fly!'

Leader Remember

Leader Remember
The time you spent
Fighting for your freedom
And that of your people
The time you played hide and go seek
With the oppressor man
Till he caught you at last
Put you in chains and leg irons
Threw you in jail
Believing in his rotten heart
That you would never again
See the light of day

Leader Remember
How strongly you fought
Your freedom-loving spirit
Kicking hard and refusing to die
Your vision for a better day
Giving you power and endurance immeasurable
In that cruel torture chamber
While your body lay on the cold cement floor
Your spirit escaped through the window
And went to mingle with other spirits
Of countless freedom fighters

Deep in Africa's rain forests
Where the Equatorial moisture whispered
That timeless message all freedom fighters know;
Don't give up
Don't give up
Here, take with you
Love
Self respect
Selflessness
Fight for your people!

Leader Remember
The day you walked out
The very minute, the very second
As your right foot stepped outside
Outside the gates of that jail
Fist in the air, sun in your face
The joy that washed over you
Like bucketfuls of honey
The pain that touched your soul
Like a poisoned arrow
Of wasted years and potential
At the same time you eagerly greeted
The mammoth task that lay ahead
You vowed and promised
To do all in your power
To build a better future for you and your people

Leader Remember
The long-suffering women and men
The dignity they lost
Think of the very young and the very old
The hunger they learnt to live with
In the land of plenty
Leader Remember
The promises you made

The hope you represent
Leader Remember
You now stand, at history's cross-roads
Compass in hand
The walking-stick of your people's experiences
Helping you feel the potholes
As you lead the way
Leader Remember, corruption and lies
Will no doubt double the pain they once knew
Please remember, betrayal hurts
Much more than the sting of a million scorpions

Leader Remember
We wish you peace in your heart
We wish you the Eagle's sharp vision
We wish you the Ancient African Tortoise's wisdom
We wish you the Mighty Elephant's memory
So Leader Remember
The Mystic Equatorial moisture whispering
That timeless message all freedom fighters know;
Don't give up
Don't give up
Here, take with you
Love
Self respect
Selflessness
Fight for your people!

PS: The fight is never over … Leader Remember …

Love Child

We Nomlambo, weNomlambo uphuma phi?
Kwaqhamuka wena, thina savuya vuya sonke . . .
Nomlambo, Nomlambo where do you come from?
You appear in our midst and suddenly we are all so happy ...

Once, a long time ago, so long ago that it is not really important to know exactly how long, there was a very beautiful village called Bhakubha. It was in a valley between two big forests. The people there had lived in that valley for hundreds of years, and their communities were bound by mutual respect and caring for one another. The rains were always good and the crops in the fields were very rich. Life in Bhakubha was so wonderful that people had almost forgotten the meaning of the words hunger and pain. For every problem, they always had a solution. It seemed as if happiness was there to stay.

But then it happened one day that a messenger brought news that another big village, not very far from Bhakubha, was declaring war on them. The news shocked and devastated everybody, but most of all the chief of Bhakubha, chief Dumile. He knew the chief of the other village very well. They were cousins who had grown up together and they still cared a lot for each other. Now, their people were fighting, and this hurt the old man very much. He became very ill and no one could tell exactly what was wrong with him. Many elders said that what he was suffering from was not only the pain of the body, but the pain of the heart. He was so ill that he could not even go with his people as they armed and set off for the battlefield. Suddenly, all the men were gone from the village of Bhakubha; only Mthunzi stayed behind, a young man who was entrusted with the task of taking care of the ailing chief Dumile.

Old women, mothers, children and the boys too young for battle remained in the village, trying to continue with their lives, trying not to worry too much about the war. But everyday, news came back from the battlefield, telling the names of the dead and injured. There was no more joy in Bhakubha. It seemed as if even the birds were singing sad songs these days. The children continued with their games, but it was not the same. The happy noises and songs that had always been a part of their childhood were no longer heard in the valley. Their mothers tried to reassure them that things would soon be better; very soon. But the children saw in their mothers' eyes a pain and despair that had never been there before. The old chief Dumile showed no signs of getting better either; it seemed as if he just wanted to die.

Then, one day, a young girl came into the village of Bhakubha. She was extraordinarily beautiful! Her face, her eyes, her smile all had a special loveliness, and there was a happy spring to the way she walked. She greeted everyone and told them that her name was Nomlambo, yes, Nomlambo. People simply stared at her, wondering where she could be from; it had been a long time since they had seen so much beauty. Her happy, carefree spirit was infectious. The village children came running to be near her. She asked them where the old women of the village were. They led her to the big round hut where the old women were sitting, working quietly. They were making grass mats, baskets, brooms and sieves. Nomlambo greeted them and told them her name. She asked if she could join them and they agreed. So she sat down right there and then and started to work. They were all impressed by the way her hands moved, so fast and neat! *Phici phici phici …*

One old woman asked, 'Hey, Nomlambo, where did you learn to work so well? Tell us please, who are your people?'

Nomlambo only smiled and said, 'Please, can you pass me some more grass?'

'But tell us, what river do you drink from, where is your home?' they asked again.

'I'm very thirsty. Can I have a sip of water to drink, please?' was her only response.

All of that day, Nomlambo sang and joked with the old women as she worked away happily. By the end of that day, when she left, still nobody knew where she had come from. They had certainly fallen in love with her and they were happy to see her return the next day. All that evening, people were talking about the beautiful girl, Nomlambo. The village girls were very jealous of the way she had got along so well with the women. The next morning when she came, the village girls were waiting for her at the entrance; 'Who does she think she is?' they asked, 'Coming into our village like this, winning the hearts of our mothers and grandmothers!'

'We also know how to make those baskets and sieves,' said one girl.

'Come on, let's show her!' challenged another.

So the village girls asked their grandmothers to please leave the big round heart for them so that they could work with Nomlambo. They sat down and got to work. The competition in that room was unbelievable! There was no singing or joking like the day before. The mothers and grandmothers peeped through the door and windows, and they found the whole thing very funny; one mother said, 'Look at our girls, working away like this! I like it; this Nomlambo should come here every day!'

The old women started to sing, a song they had made up especially for Nomlambo.

'Wee Nomlambo, wee Nomlambo uphuma phi na,
Kwaqhamuka wena, savuya vuya sonke . . .'

The song simply said:

'Nomlambo, where have you come from?

You come here and we are suddenly so very happy ...'

But the girls were far from happy. They especially disliked the way Nomlambo was so quick and good at her work. At the end of the day, when she left the village, the young boys were waiting to follow her home, to see where she came from.

'I just love the way she walks; have you seen those lovely legs?' one boy said.

'It's her eyes that get me; those eyes seem to hold far-away secrets,' said another.

'No, it's the lips that kill me; that smile is like a rising sun that dawns again and again,' said a third, growing all dreamy.

Then they saw Nomlambo leaving the village. The boys chased after her. But she was running much too fast. She outran them as though they were little children. Her feet hardly seemed to touch the ground as she disappeared in the distance. The boys came back to the village huffing and puffing. The girls looked at them crossly and said:

'We are here, so why do you have to chase that strange Nomlambo?'

The boys simply grumbled and went to rest for the remainder of the day.

News travelled all over the village about that very beautiful girl, Nomlambo. Mthunzi, the young man who was taking care of the chief, also heard about her and was curious to meet her. He sat under a tree at the entrance to the village early the next morning. He saw her coming and looked the other way. She walked right past him and he did not even greet her. She stopped and retraced her steps.

'Sawubona, Bhuti,' she greeted him, smiling coyly.

'Yebo,' Mthunzi greeted back.

'My name is Nomlambo, what's yours?'

'Mthunzi,' he said.

'Oh Mthunzi, that is a lovely name. Can I sit with you?' she asked.

So there they sat, talking and laughing, getting to know

one another. That day, Nomlambo did not go to work in the big round hut, but stayed with Mthunzi, even for the midday meal. Soon, people were talking, saying all kinds of things about Nomlambo.

'Look at her, taking Mthunzi away from his duties. He is supposed to be taking care of the chief, you know.'

'I suspect she is a spy from the other village that is fighting with our people. Otherwise, why won't she say where her home is?'

'Look at the way everyone seems to fall in love with her the moment they meet her! There is some witchcraft in this, one way or the other . . .'

But the old women saw how happy Mthunzi was with Nomlambo and they sang their song again:

'Wee Nomlambo, wee Nomlambo uphuma phi na?
Kwaqhamuka wena savuya vuya sonke . . .'

When Nomlambo left that afternoon, Mthunzi smiled and said goodbye. He did not try to follow her.

The next day, Nomlambo did not look for the old women and the big round hut, she simply went straight to where Mthunzi was waiting for her. They sat and talked, took walks together and had a really wonderful day. At the end of that day, Mthunzi was ready. When she said goodbye, he said:

'Let me walk you to that hill over there.'

When they got to that point, he said:

'Oh, let me walk you to that big tree over there.'

When they got to that tree, Mthunzi said: 'You know, I just hate to think that you will walk through this forest alone. Let me walk you through to the other side and then I'll have to really say goodbye.'

But when they got to the other side, Nomlambo knew that Mthunzi was not planning to let her go. So she started to run, just as fast as she could. But Mthunzi was right there behind her. She ran faster and so did he. After a long time of running, they came to a big river with a deep pool, where the water was almost green because of its depth. Nomlambo jumped in – '*Qumbu!*' – with the water splashing in every direction. And '*Qumbu!*' – into the water Mthunzi followed. They swam down, down until they got to a cave under the deep pool. It was dry and they could actually stand. While Mthunzi was looking around to see where he was, he suddenly heard the sound of a drum. He looked to see where that sound was coming from. There were five old women playing a big round drum, with a rhythm and melody he had never heard before. He was enchanted by their skilled hands and the whole atmosphere in that cave. He wished so much to play too, and he wondered if they would let him.

As if they had read his mind, one of them beckoned to Mthunzi to come forward. He went and sat with them. Slowly, he picked up the rhythm. The more he played, the better his playing became. He played louder and louder, not wanting to stop, completely taken over by this wonderful new rhythm; he even closed his eyes. So he did not notice that the old women had all stood up and left him; until he stopped playing. He hardly had time to wonder about anything before Nomlambo reappeared from behind a rock. She had changed into new clothes. She wore a beautiful buckskin skirt, a bright red beaded necklace and bracelet. She also had *chigers* – ankle rattles or shakers – on her feet. Her hair was decorated with beads and shells and she looked much more beautiful than Mthunzi had ever imagined possible. He rose to meet her. He was about to touch her hand when the old women returned, looking very serious this time. One of them was carrying a leather pouch, which she handed to Mthunzi, saying,

'Take this. Inside, there are roots and herbs. Take them to your ailing chief, boil them up and let him drink the medicine. He will be better in no time.'

'And this drum that you have learnt to play so well,' said another, 'take it with you to the battlefield tonight. Go and stop that war!' Her commanding voice was almost a shout.

Mthunzi did not waste any time. He thanked the mysterious old women and took the drum. He was headed for the exit when Nomlambo said, 'I'm going with him.'

The women nodded without surprise. Of course they had known that was coming. They waved the pair goodbye as they swam up to the top of the pool.

When Mthunzi and Nomlambo emerged from the water, they saw that the full moon had come up. It was round and bright, shining in the shimmering water like a giant eye, as if to witness this very important evening. Mthunzi took this as a sign of good luck

Nomlambo took Mthunzi's hand and they ran all the way through the forest and to the village. At the chief's home, they made the medicine for him to drink. Then Mthunzi left Nomlambo with the old man, asking her to take special care of him.

He took the big round drum to the battlefield. It was midnight by the time he got there. He sat down in a spot that seemed to be on neutral ground. He began to play the drum; slowly at first. Then, he played louder and louder, until that magical rhythm was reverberating throughout the countryside. All the soldiers woke up. The soldiers from Mthunzi's village shouted:

'Did you hear that drum? Why are those cowards attacking in the middle of the night? Well, we will show them; *Ayihlome!* – let us arm ourselves.' They got ready to fight and defend themselves.

The soldiers from the other side were thinking the same thing.

'How dare they attack in the middle of the night when everyone is sleeping! We will teach them a lesson, each and every one of them. Such cowards; *Ayihlome!*'

They set off to fight. But as they got closer and closer to the fighting area, each group realised that the soldiers from the other side were not the ones playing the drum. In fact, they could feel that this rhythm was new and different. Soon, they found themselves moving to the rhythm of the drum. The longer that the drum played, the more they felt it pounding inside their hearts. Their spears fell, one after the other, and it did not even matter. They were moving to the rhythm of the drum. Shields began to fall too and no one cared. They were moving to the rhythm of the drum. A soldier felt the touch of another's hand and they held onto each other, as they continued to dance to the new music. By now, they had formed a large circle of dancing warriors. They made a marvellous sight under the bright moonlight. They all kept their eyes fixed on the drum, until Mthunzi stopped playing.

Then the men suddenly started talking to one another noisily, introducing themselves to those they did not know.

'Mfowethu, I do not know you; I am Zondo, who are you?'

'Dlamini? You don't say! My wife is Madlamini.'

'And you look so much like the Thabethe people; am I right? He-he, I knew it!'

And then one of the very respected generals stopped and picked up a shield. He looked at it and said, 'This shield; I could work on it, wet it for a while and then I am sure I can make myself a beautiful drum from it, almost as magical as the one this young man was playing.'

Another soldier picked up a spear and said, 'This spear, I could work on it, melt it and reshape it till it makes a beautiful serving spoon for my mother. I miss her morning porridge!'

Soon different men were finding different uses for their weapons, and they all knew that the war had come to an end.

Mthunzi, his job done, picked up the drum, put it on his shoulder and headed back home. He was walking as fast as he could. His heart was pounding and he was longing to see Nomlambo again. Now, he was very sure that he loved her with all his heart. The soldiers from his village said goodbye to their new friends and followed the young man with the drum.

When they got back home, there was much ululation and celebration as the whole village woke up to the most glorious news of all. The war was over! People got back to their peaceful lives and were glad to see their chief well again.

From that time on, always in January, when the moon was

full, the two villages came together on the battlefield; not to fight this time, but to celebrate, to sing and dance and play many, many drums. Some of the songs they sang were in praise of Nomlambo, the 'love child' as the old women called her.

Needless to say, she and Mthunzi got married and lived a happy life. All were thankful for the magic drum from the cave under the river – the drum that had stopped a senseless war.

A Brighter Dawn for African Women

Hoyiiii-na! Hoyina!!
Everybody come out and watch
Today the morning star shines brighter
As it triumphantly ushers in the sunrise
The day has finally dawned when
The African woman
Will be appreciated and honoured for who she really is
For hundreds of years hunger and disease
Have been her unwanted companions
Denied education and the dignity every woman deserves
As insults and humiliation were heaped upon her
All too often made to feel like a refugee in her own home
She has been fighting the battles of colonialism
One after the other, without any recognition

But you would not say so by the smile she bears
To kiss the sunrise each morning
Grateful just to be alive with her children and man
Her laughter inspires birds to sing new melodies
She hates war with all her heart
Every time she's called upon to sing and dance for one victory
Her hips sway longingly for all wars to end

For every bullet on the African soil
To turn to a ripe juicy fruit
A vegetable seed or a cup of creamy milk
The woman of Africa wants to sing a song of love
To bring back old wisdoms that will shine a new light
Brighter than the stars in the night sky
For all her tears and laughter, her wishes and endeavours
May all the springs, lakes and rivers, sing her praises
Every single day so she may not tire
May the leaves of every tree sing Halala! Halala!
We celebrate you, Woman of Africa
Halala! Halala! We celebrate you!!